Umboo, the Elephant

Howard Roger Garis

Umboo, the Elephant

CHAPTER I

BABY UMBOO

"Oh, my! But it's hot! It is just too hot for anything!" cried Chako, one of the monkeys in the circus cage. "It is hotter under this tent than ever it was in the jungle! Whew!" and he hung by his tail and swung to and fro from a wooden bar.

"In the jungle we could find a pool of water where we could keep cool," said another monkey, who was poking around the floor of the cage, hoping he could find a peanut. But there were only shells. "I wish I could go back to the jungle," he chattered.

"What did you come away from the jungle for, if you don't like it in this circus?" asked Woo-Uff, the big yellow lion, who lay on his back in his cage, his legs stuck up in the air, for he was cooler that way. "Why did you come from the jungle, Chako?"

"I didn't want to come," answered the swinging monkey. "But some white and black hunters caught me, and a lot more of us chattering chaps, and took us away from the jungle."

"That's right, my boy!" exclaimed the deep, rumbly voice of Umboo, the biggest elephant in the circus. "None of us animals would have come away from the jungle if we could have had our way. But, now that we are here, we must make the best of it."

"How can one make the best of it when it is so hot?" asked Chako. "The sun shines down on this circus tent hotter than ever it did in the jungle. And there is no pool of water where we can splash and be cool."

"Oh, if water is all you want, I can give you some of that," spoke

Umboo. "Wait a minute!"

Near the elephants, of whom Umboo was one on a long line, chained to stakes driven in the ground, was a big tub of water, put there for them to drink when they wanted to. Umboo put his long, rubbery hose of a trunk down into this tub of water, and sucked up a lot, just as you fill your rubber ball at the bathroom basin.

"Look out now, monkeys!" cried the elephant. "It's going to rain!" and he sort of laughed away down in his throat. He couldn't laugh through his nose, as his nose was his trunk, and that was full of water. "Look out for a shower!" he cried.

With that the elephant went:

"Woof-umph!"

Out from his trunk, as if from a hose, sprinkled a shower of water. Over the cage of monkeys it sprayed, wetting them as might a fall of rain.

"Here comes some more!" cried Umboo, and again he dipped his trunk in the tub of water, sucked up some in the two hollow places, and again squirted it over the monkeys' cage.

"Oh, that's good! That's fine!" cried Chako. "That was like being in a jungle rain. I'm cooler now. Squirt some more, Umboo!"

"No, hold on, if you please!" rumbled another elephant. "It is all right for Umboo to splatter some water on you poor monkeys, but if he quirts away all in the tub we will have none to drink."

"That's so," said Umboo. "I can't squirt away all the water, Chako. We big elephants have to drink a lot more than you little monkeys. But when the circus men fill our tub again, I'll squirt some more on you."

"Thank you!" chattered Chako. "I feel cooler, anyhow. And we monkeys can't stand too much water. This felt fine!"

The monkeys in the cage were quite damp, and some began combing out their long hair with their queer little fingers, that look almost like yours, except that their thumb isn't quite the same.

"If Umboo can't squirt any more water on us, maybe he can do something else to help us forget that it is so hot," said Gink, a funny little monkey, who had a very long tail.

"What can he do, except squirt water on us?" asked Chako. "And I wish he'd do that again. It's the only thing to make us cooler."

"No, I wasn't thinking of that, though I do like a little water," spoke Gink. "But don't you remember, Umboo, you promised to tell us a story of how you lived in a jungle when you were a baby elephant?"

"Oh, yes, so he did!" exclaimed Chako. "I had forgotten about that. It will make us cooler, I think, to hear you tell a story, Umboo. Please do!"

"Well, all right, I will," said the big elephant, as he swung to and fro; because elephants are very seldom still, but always moving as they stand. And they sleep standing up—did you know that?

"I'll tell you a story about my jungle," went on Umboo. "But perhaps you will not like it as well as you did the story Snarlie the tiger told you."

"Oh, yes we will," said Snarlie himself, a big, handsome striped tiger in a cage not far from where the monkeys lived. "You can tell us a good story, Umboo."

"And make it as long as the story Woo-Uff, the lion, told us," begged

Humpo, the camel. "I liked his story."

"Thank you," spoke Woo-Uff, as he rolled over near the edge of his cage where he could hear better. "I'm glad you liked my story, Humpo, but I'm sure Umboo's will be better than mine. And don't forget the funny part, my big elephant friend."

"What funny part is that?" asked Horni, the rhinoceros.

"Oh, I guess he means where I once filled my trunk with water and squirted some on a man, as I did on the monkeys just now," said the swaying elephant.

"Why did you do that?" Chako wanted to know.

"Well, I'll tell you when I get to that part of my story," said the elephant. "Now do you all want to hear me talk?"

"Oh, yes! yes!" cried the animals in the circus tent. "Tell us your story, Umboo! Tell us about when you were a baby in the far-off jungle of Africa."

"I did not come from Africa; I came from an Indian jungle," said Umboo. "My friends, the African elephants, are much larger than I am, and they are wilder and fiercer, and so they are hardly every caught for the circus."

"I remember a great big elephant in a circus I was once with — not this one, though," said Humpo, the camel. "His name was Jug — no it was not Jug, and it wasn't Jig, but it began with a J."

"Maybe it was Jumbo," suggested Umboo.

"That was it — Jumbo!" cried Humpo. "He was a very big elephant."

"Yes, I guess he was," said Umboo. "I have heard of him, but I never saw him. He was an African elephant, and they are all large. Poor Jumbo!"

"Why do you say that?" asked Chako the monkey. "Poor Jumbo?"

"Because he is dead," said Umboo. "Poor Jumbo was struck by one of those big puffing animals, of steam and steel and iron, that pull our circus train over the shiny rails."

"You mean a choo-choo-locomotive-steam-engine," said Woo-Uff, the lion.

"I suppose that is the name," said Umboo. "Anyhow, Jumbo was hit by an engine, and, big as he was, it killed him. His bones, or skeleton, are in a museum in New York now."

"Is New York a jungle?" asked Gink, who had not been with the circus very long.

"New York a jungle? Of course not!" laughed Snarlie, the tiger. "New York is a big city, and sometimes we circus animals are taken there to help with the show. I've been in New York lots of times."

"Well, don't let it make you proud," said Chako, the other monkey. "I have been there myself, and I'd much rather be in the jungle."

"Say, are we going to listen to you animals talk or hear the story Umboo is going to tell us?" asked Humpo, the camel. "I thought he was going to make us forget the heat."

"So I am," said Umboo, in a kind voice, "Only I wanted to speak about old Jumbo, There used to be a song about him, many years ago. It went something like this, and I heard a little English boy sing it:

"Alice said to Jumbo:

'I love you!'

Jumbo said to Alice:

'I don't believe you do;

'Cause if you love me truly,

As you say you do,

Come over to America

To Barnum's show!'"

"That's the song they used to sing about Jumbo, more than twenty years ago," said Umboo.

"My! How can you remember so far back?" asked Chako.

"Oh, we elephants live to a good old age," said Umboo. "Why, I am fifty years old now, and yet I am young! Some of the elephants in the jungle lived to be a hundred and twenty years old!"

"Oh, my!" cried Chako. "Did they have circuses as long ago as that?"

"Yes, but not the kind that traveled about, and showed in white tents," said Umboo. "But I have heard my father and mother say that we elephants live to be very old."

"And can you remember so far back, when you were a baby in the jungle?" asked Humpo.

"Oh, yes, very easily," answered Umboo. "I am going to tell you a story about how first I was a little elephant in the great, green forest, or jungle, and then I'll tell you how I was caught, and worked in a lumber yard in India, and how I was then sold to a circus."

"Well, then, please begin!" begged Chako. "It is getting hot again in this monkey cage, and if you haven't any water to squirt on us tell us your story."

"I will!" promised the elephant. And then, as the afternoon show was over, and it was not yet time for the night one to begin, the animals had a little quiet time to themselves. And, as they had done once before, they got ready to listen to a story.

In the book before this I have written for you the story of Woo-Uff, the lion. And before that I gave you the story of Snarlie, the tiger. And now we come to Umboo.

"The first thing I remember," began the elephant, "was when I was a little baby in the jungle."

"Were you very little?" asked Snarlie the tiger.

"Well, I have heard my mother say I weighed about two hundred pounds the first day I came into the world," answered Umboo. "So, though I was little for an elephant, I would have made a very big monkey, I suppose. And for a time I just stayed near my mother, between her two, big front legs, so the other elephants would not step on me, and I drank the milk my mother gave me, for my teeth were not yet ready for me to chew roots, leaves and grass."

"Tell us something that happened!" begged Chako, "and make it exciting, so we will forget about the heat!"

"Well," said Umboo, "I'll tell you of a terrible fright we had, and how — "

But just then something else happened. Into the tent came running one of the circus men, and he cried to another, who was asleep on some hay near the elephants.

"Come! Loosen Umboo! We need him to help us get one of the wagons out of the mud! Bring Umboo, the strongest of all elephants!"

CHAPTER II

ON THE MARCH

Umboo, the big circus elephant, was unchained from the stake in the circus tent to which he was made fast, and led out by one of the men.

"Oh, where are you going?" asked Horni, the rhinoceros, who had been taking a little doze, and who woke up, just as the men came in. "I thought I heard some one say you were going to tell a story, Umboo," spoke the rhinoceros.

"I was going to, and I started it," the elephant answered, "but now I must go out and help push a wagon loose from where it is stuck in the mud. I'll be back pretty soon, for it is no trouble at all for me to push even a big circus wagon."

"Yes, you are very strong," said Chako, the monkey. "Well, don't forget to come back and tell us about the jungle. That will make us forget the heat."

"Come, Umboo!" called one of the men, as he loosed the heavy elephant chains. "You must help us with the wagon."

Out of the circus tent walked the big elephant. He could understand some of the things the circus men said to him, just as your dog can understand you, when you call:

"Come here, Jack!" Then he runs to you, wagging his tail. But if you say:

"Go on home, Jack!"

How his tail droops, and how sadly your dog looks at you, even though you know it is best for him to go back, and not, perhaps, go to school with you, like Mary's little lamb.

So, in much the same way, Umboo knew what the men wanted of him. He was led across the circus lot, outside the big, white tent, that was gay with many-colored flags, and as Umboo swayed along, some boys, who were watching for what they might see, caught sight of the great elephant.

"Hey, Jim! Here's one of the big ones!" shouted one boy.

"Maybe he's going to take a drink out of the canal," said another.

"Maybe they're going to give him a swim," spoke a third boy.

But the men had something else for Umboo to do just then. They led him to where one of the big wagons, covered with red and gold paint, and shiny with pieces of looking glass, was stuck fast in the mud on a hill. For it had rained the day before the circus came to show in the town, and the ground was soft.

"Now, Umboo!" called the circus man, who was really one of the elephant keepers, and who gave them food and water, "now, Umboo, let us see if you can get this wagon out of the mud, as you did once before. The horses can not pull it, but you are stronger than many horses."

The horses, with red plumes on their heads, were still hitched to the wagon. There were eight of them, but they had pulled and pulled, and still the wagon was stuck in the mud.

"Are you going to help us, Umboo?" asked one of the horses who knew the elephant, for the circus animals can talk among themselves, just as you boys and girls do. "Are you going to help us?"

"I am going to try," Umboo answered. "You look tired, horsies! Take a

little rest now, while I look and see which is the best way to push.

Then, when I blow through my nose like a trumpet horn, you pull and

I'll push, and we'll have the wagon out of the mud very soon!"

Umboo was led up to the back of the wagon. He looked at where the wheels were sunk away down in the soft ground, and then, being the strongest and most wise of all the beasts of the world, the elephant put his big, broad head against the wagon.

"Now, then, horsies! Pull!" he cried, trumpeting through his trunk, which was hollow like a hose. "Pull, horsies!"

The horses pulled and Umboo, the elephant, pushed, and soon the wagon was out on firm, hard ground.

"That's good!" cried the circus man. "I knew Umboo could do it!"

Then he gave the elephant a sweet bun, which he had saved for him, and back to the tent went Umboo.

"Now, please go on with your story!" begged Chako. "Tell us what happened in the jungle."

"I will," said Umboo, and this is the story he told. Umboo was only one of a number of baby elephants that lived with their fathers and mothers in the deep, green jungles of India. Not like the other jungle beasts were the elephants, for the big animals had no regular home. They did not live in caves as did the lions and tigers, for no cave was large enough for a herd of elephants.

And, except in the case of solitary, or lonely elephants, which are often savage beasts, or "rogues," all elephants live in herds—a number of them always keeping together, just like a herd of cows.

Another reason why elephants do not live in one place, like a lion's cave, or in a nest or lair under the thick grass where a tiger brings up her striped babies, is that elephants eat so much that they have to keep moving from place to place to get more food.

They will eat all there is in one part of the jungle, and then travel many miles to a new place, not coming back to the first one until there are more green leaves, fresh grass, or new bark on the trees which they have partly stripped.

So Umboo, the two-hundred-pound baby elephant, lived with his mother in the jungle, drinking nothing but milk for the first six months, as he had no teeth to chew even the most tender grass.

"Well, are you strong enough to walk along now?" Umboo's mother asked him one day in the jungle, and this was when he was about half a week old.

"Oh, yes, I can walk now," said the baby elephant, as he swayed to and fro between his mother's front legs, while she stood over him to keep the other big elephants, and some of the half-grown elephant boys and girls, from bumping into him, and knocking him over. "I can walk all right. But why do you ask me that?" Umboo wanted to know.

"Because the herd is going to march away," said Mrs. Stumptail, which was the name of Umboo's mother. "They are going to march to another part of the jungle, and your father and I will march with them, as we do not want to be left behind. There is not much more left here to eat. We have taken all the palm nuts and leaves from the trees. We have only been waiting until you grew strong enough to march."

"Oh, I can march all right," said Umboo, telling his story to the circus animals in the tent. "Look how fast I can go!"

Out he started from under his mother's body, striding across a grassy place in the jungle. But Umboo was not as good at walking as he had thought. Even though he weighed two hundred pounds his legs were not very strong, and soon he began to totter.

"Look out!" cried his mother. "You are going to fall!" and she reached out her trunk and wound it around Umboo, holding him up.

"Hello!" trumpeted Mr. Stumptail, coming up just then with a big green branch in his trunk. "What's the matter here?"

"Umboo was just showing me how well he could walk," said his mother, speaking elephant talk, of course. "I told him the herd would soon be on the march, and that he must come along."

"But we won't go until he is strong enough," said Umboo's father. "Here," he said to Mrs. Stumptail, "eat this branch of palm nuts. They are good and sweet. Eat them while I go and see Old Tusker. I'll tell him not to start to lead the herd to another part of the jungle until Umboo is stronger."

Then, giving the mother elephant a branch of palm nuts, which food the big jungle animals like best of all, Mr. Stumptail went to see Tusker, the oldest and largest elephant of the jungle—he who always led the herd on the march.

"My new little boy elephant is not quite strong enough to march, yet," said Mr. Stumptail to Tusker. "Can we wait here another day or two?"

"Oh, yes, of course, Mr. Stumptail," said the kind, old head elephant. "You know the herd will never go faster than the mothers and baby elephants can travel."

And this is true, as any old elephant hunter will tell you.

"Thank you," said Mr. Stumptail, to Tusker; for elephants are polite to each other, even though, in the jungle, they sometimes may be a bit rough toward lions and tigers, of whom they are afraid.

Back to the mother elephant and Baby Umboo went Mr. Stumptail, to tell them there was no hurry about the herd marching away. And two or three days later Umboo had grown stronger and was not so wobbly on his legs. He could run about a little, and once he even tried to bump his head against another elephant boy, quite older than he was.

"Here! You mustn't do that!" cried his mother. "What trick are you up to now?"

"Well, this elephant laughed at your tail," said Umboo. "He said it was a little short one, and not long like his mother's!"

"Don't mind that!" said Mrs. Stumptail, with a sort of laugh away down in her trunk. "All our family have short, or stumpy tails. That is how we get our name. The Stumptail elephants are very stylish, let me tell you."

"Oh, then it's all right," said Umboo, who was called by that name because he had made that sort of noise or sound through his nose, when he was a day old. And elephants and jungle folk are named for the sort of noises they make, or for something they do, or look like, just as Indians are named.

So Umboo played in the deep jungle forest with the other little elephant boys and girls until his mother and father saw that he was strong enough to walk well by himself.

"Now we will start on a long march!" called Tusker one day. "The jungle here is well eaten, and, besides, it is no longer safe for us here. So we will march."

"Why isn't the jungle safe here any more?" asked Umboo of his mother.

"I'll tell you," answered Tusker, who heard what the little elephant asked. "The other day," went on the big chap, "I went to the top of the hill over there," and he pointed with his trunk. "I heard up there a noise like thunder, but it was not thunder."

"What was it?" asked Umboo, who liked to listen to the talk of the old herd-leader. The other little elephants also gathered around to listen.

"It was the noise of the guns of the hunters," said Tusker. "They are

coming to our jungle, and where the hunters come is no place for us.

So we must march away and hide. Also there is not much food left here.

We must go to a new jungle-place."

Raising his trunk in the air Tusker gave a loud call. All the other elephants gathered around him, and off he started, leading the way through the green forest.

"Now if I go too fast for any of you baby elephants, just squeak and I'll stop," said the big, kind elephant. "We will go only as fast as you little chaps can walk."

"You are very kind," said Mrs. Stumptail, helping Umboo, with her trunk, to get over a rough bit of ground.

On and on marched the elephants to find a new place in the jungle, where they would be safe from the hunters, and where they could find more sweet bark, leaves and palm nuts to eat. Umboo walked near his mother, as the other small elephant boys and girls walked near their mothers, and the bigger elephants helped the smaller and weaker ones over the rough places.

Pretty soon, in the jungle, the herd of elephants came to what seemed a big silver ribbon, shining in the sun. It sparkled like a looking glass on a circus wagon, though, as yet, neither Umboo, nor any of the other big animals had ever seen a show.

"What is that?" asked Umboo of his mother.

"That is a river of water," she answered. "It is water to drink and wash in."

"Oh, I never could drink all that water," said the baby elephant.

"No one expects you to!" said his mother, with an elephant laugh. "But we are going to swim across it to get on the other side."

"What is swimming?" asked Umboo.

"It means going in the water, and wiggling your legs so that you will float across and not sink," said Mrs. Stumptail. "See, we are at the jungle river now, and we will go across."

"Oh, but I'm afraid!" cried Umboo, holding back. "I don't want to go in all that water."

Mrs. Stumptail reached out her trunk and caught her little boy around the middle of his stomach.

"You must do as I tell you!" she said. "Up you go!" and she lifted him high in the air.

"Oh, did she let you fall?" suddenly asked Chako, who, with the other animals in the circus tent, was eagerly listening to the story Umboo was telling. "Did she let you fall?"

CHAPTER III

SLIDING DOWN HILL

"Look here!" cried Snarlie, the tiger, when Chako, the monkey, had asked his question. "Look here, Chako! You mustn't interrupt like that when Umboo is talking! Let him tell his story, just as you let me tell mine. And maybe Umboo's jungle story will go in a book, as mine did."

"Is yours in a book?" asked Humpo, the camel.

"It is," answered Snarlie, and he did not speak at all proudly as some tigers might. "My story is in a book, and there are pictures of me, and also Toto, the little Indian princess. For I came from India, just as Umboo did."

"Now who is talking?" asked Woo-Uff, the lion. "I thought we were to listen to Umboo's story."

"That's right—we were," said Snarlie. "I'm sorry I talked so much.

But I was telling Chako about the books we are in, Woo-Uff."

"Yes, books are all well enough," said the lion, "but give me a good piece of meat. Now go on, Umboo. What was it Chako asked?"

"I wanted to know if Umboo's mother let him fall when she lifted him high up in her trunk when they came to the jungle river," said the monkey in the circus cage.

"No," answered Umboo, "she did not drop me. My mother was very strong, and her trunk had a good hold of me. She didn't drop me at all."

"Then what did she lift you up for?" asked Chako. "Once, in the jungle where I came from, I saw a big elephant lift up a tiger in his trunk, and the elephant threw the tiger down on the ground as hard as he could, and hurt him."

"That was because the tiger was going to bite the elephant if he could," answered Umboo. "Elephants only have their tusks, and trunk and big feet to fight with. They can't bite as you monkeys can, nor as lions and tigers can. But my mother lifted me up in her trunk to put me on her back."

"What did she want to do that for?" asked Humpo, the camel. "Was a hunter coming with a gun?"

"No, but she was going to swim across the river with the rest of the herd," answered Umboo, "and she knew I was too little to know how to swim yet. I learned how later, though, and I liked the water. But this time my mother took me across the river on her back."

"It's a good thing your mother didn't have a camel-back like Humpo," said Woo-Uff, with a sort of chuckling laugh.

"Why?" asked Horni, the rhinoceros.

"Because, if Mrs. Stumptail had a back, with humps in, as the camels have, Umboo would have fallen off into the water," said the lion, as he opened his big mouth in a sleepy yawn, showing his big, white, sharp teeth.

"My mother's back was big and strong," said Umboo. "It was flat, and not humpy, like a camel's, though their backs are all right on the desert. My mother lifted me up on her back with her trunk, and there I sat while she and the other elephants waded into the river."

And then the circus elephant went on telling his story.

Into the jungle river walked the elephants, the littlest ones on their mothers' backs, and some, very small ones, held in their mothers' trunks, which were lifted high in the air. These were the babies of the herd who were too small to ride safely on the backs of the big creatures.

"Pooh! I'm bigger than you! I can swim like the other elephants!" said Keedah; a large elephant boy, as he looked up and saw Umboo on his mother's back. "I don't have to be carried across a river! I can swim by myself."

"And so will my little boy, soon," said Mrs. Stumptail. "Swim on your own side, Keedah, and don't splash water on Umboo."

But Keedah was a little elephant chap full of mischief, and he did not do as he was told. Instead he filled his trunk with water and sprayed it all over Umboo.

"Ouch!" cried the little elephant baby, for the water felt cold, at first. "Stop it, Keedah!"

"Ha! Ha! I made you get wet, whether you swim or not!" laughed Keedah.

"I'll put some more water on you!"

"No you don't! Now you swim along!" suddenly cried Mrs. Stumptail.

"Get away!"

With that she tapped Keedah on his head with her trunk two or three times, and, when an elephant wants to, it can strike very hard with its long nose, even though it seems soft.

"Ouch! Ouch!" trumpeted Keedah as he swam out of reach of Mrs.

Stumptail. "Ouch! Let me alone!"

"Learn to behave yourself then," said Umboo's mother.

"I'm going to tell my father on you!" cried the mischievous little elephant.

"Well, it won't do you any good," said a heavy voice behind him, and there was Keedah's father himself swimming along. "I saw what you did to Umboo," went on the old gentleman elephant, "and Mrs. Stumptail did just right to tap you with her trunk. Now be a good boy, and don't shower any more water on the baby elephants."

So Keedah promised that he wouldn't, and Umboo clung as tightly as he could, with his sprawly legs, to his mother's broad back as she swam across the river.

The water was wide, at this part of the jungle, but elephants are good swimmers. They can go in very deep water, and as long as they can keep the tip end of their trunk out, so they can breathe, the rest of their body can sink away down below the surface. And when the elephants are in the water the flies, mosquitoes and other biting bugs of the jungle can not harm them.

For, though the skin of elephants, rhinoceros beasts, and even the hippopotami, is very thick, some bugs can bite through it enough to give pain, and the animals don't like that. But in the water nothing can bite them, unless it's a crocodile, and none of those big fellows would come near a whole herd of elephants.

"What are we going to do when we get on the other side of the river?" asked Umboo of his mother, as he reached his trunk down in the water and took a little drink.

"Oh, we will rest a while, eat something, perhaps, and then we will keep on marching to a better part of the jungle," she answered.

"I know what I'm going to do when I get on the other shore," spoke

Keedah, as once more he swam up along side of Umboo and his mother.

"What?" asked the little elephant who was having such a nice ride across the river. "What are you going to do?"

"I am going to have a slide down hill," went on Keedah, who did not seem to be going to make any more trouble.

"What's sliding down hill?" asked Umboo, and of course, you understand, all this talk was in animal language.

"Sliding down hill is fun," went on Keedah. "You know Old Tusker went up to the top of a place, called a hill, to look and see about the hunters in the jungle. Well, there is a hill on the other side of this river, and when we get across I'm going to the top of it and slide down.

"It's hard work going up hill," went on the larger elephant boy, "but it's easy coming down. You just sit on your hind legs, hold your trunk up in the air and down you come as fast as anything!"

"And be careful you don't bump into anything," said Mrs. Stumptail. "Sliding down hill is all right if you don't bump into anything. You must be careful, Umboo. Don't slide down any hills unless you ask me first."

"I won't," promised the baby elephant. "But tell me more about it,

Keedah. Did you ever slide down hill?"

"Many a time. I was with the herd last year when we swam this same river. I could swim then, too, and when we came to the hill I climbed up. Then I came down lots faster than I walked up, and I went splash into the river. That didn't hurt at all," he said to Umboo's mother.

"No, it doesn't hurt to slide into the water," said the old elephant lady. "If you do any sliding, Umboo, see that you splash into the water, and not on the hard ground."

"I will, after I learn to swim," spoke Umboo.

A little later the herd of elephants were safely across the jungle river. Some rested in the shade of trees, pulling off the low branches and the palm nuts. Others rolled in the mud, to make a sort of coating over their skins, to keep off the flies. Others went to the top of the hill to slide down, and Keedah went with them.

"Oh, mother! I wish I could slide!" said Umboo, when he saw what fun the other elephants were having. They really did slide down hill, just as otters do, only the otter, or beaver, likes to have water on his slide, and the elephants did not care whether their slide was wet or dry. Down they came, over sticks and stones, and their skin was so tough that they never got hurt. And yet a fly could bite through that same hide! But that is because a fly has a very fine, sharp bill, which can go through the tiny pores, or holes, in the elephant's skin.

"Oh, I want to slide!" said Umboo to his mother. "I'm big enough, and if I can't swim when I splash in the water, you can be near to pull me out. Please let me slide down hill!"

"And did she let you?" asked Snarlie, the tiger, as the elephant stopped in the telling his story long enough to take a bite of hay. "Did she let you, Umboo?"

CHAPTER IV

UMBOO LEARNS SOMETHING

Umboo, the big circus elephant, swallowed the sweet hay he had been chewing, and was about to keep on with the telling of his story about the things that happened to him when he was a little chap in the Indian jungle, when a lot of men came in the tent where the animals were standing about, or resting in their cages.

"Oh, now we can't hear any more of the story," said Chako, the big monkey, to Gink the little, long-tailed chap.

"Why can't we?" Gink wanted to know.

"Because the circus is going to move on. Our cage will be put on the steam cars, and away we will go, and Umboo, and the rest of the elephants, will be put in big box-cars."

"Won't we ever see him again, or hear more of his story?" asked Gink, who had not been with the circus very long, and so did not know much about it.

"Oh, yes, of course we'll hear more later on," answered Chako, "but not until tomorrow. Now the circus is going to move."

And that is just what happened. The men closed the sides of the cages, shutting the animals up in them. The tent was taken down, horses were hitched to the wagons, and away went the whole, big circus on a train to the next town where the show was to be given.

"It's too bad!" exclaimed Horni, the rhinoceros, who had a big horn on the end of his nose. "It's too bad, Umboo! I wanted to hear you tell about sliding down hill."

"I'll tell you tomorrow," said the elephant. "Now I have to go and help the horses, by pushing on some of the heavy wagons with my head. I'll finish the sliding-down-hill part of my story tomorrow."

"All right, don't forget!" called Chako, just before the men closed down the sides of the monkey cage.

"I won't," promised Umboo.

"It was the same way when I was telling my story," said Snarlie, the tiger. "Every now and then I had to stop when the circus moved from one place to another."

All through the night the trains of cars, with the circus wagons, tents, horses and performers, rolled along. In the morning the cars stopped just outside a big city, where the show was to be given for three days.

"And now I'll have a chance to tell you a lot more about what we elephants did in the jungle," said Umboo, when, once more, all the animal friends were in the tent together. "That is I'll tell you more, if you aren't tired of hearing it," he added.

"Tired? I should say not!" chattered Gink. "Go on, Umboo, if you please. Tell us a lot more!"

"And don't forget about sliding down hill," added Woo-Uff, the lion.

"Did your mother let you?"

"Oh, yes, she let me," answered Umboo. "At first she did not want to, for a lot of the big elephants were having this fun. But, after a while, when they went away from the hill, having slid down enough, and when Keedah, and some of the other elephant boys and girls, took their turn, I went with them.

"At first I was a little afraid, when I got to the top of the hill, and saw how steep it was, and how far it seemed down to the bottom where the river ran. But I stuck my front feet out in front of me, and I sat down on the back part of my hind legs, where my skin is very thick, and then, all of a sudden Keedah came up behind me and gave me a push." "Did you go down?" asked Snarlie, laughing so that his sharp, white teeth showed in his red mouth.

"Did I go down? I should say I did!" cried Umboo. "I went down so fast I almost turned over in a somersault, the way the trick dogs do in our circus. And, at first, I was scared.

"But the hill of dirt was smooth, without any big stones in it, and away I slid. When I got to the water, in I went with a big splash; though of course I didn't make as much of a splatter as some of the larger elephants did."

"Was it fun?" asked Humpo, the camel.

"At first I didn't like it," answered Umboo. "The water got up my trunk, and choked me a little, and took my breath away. But my mother stood on the bank of the river and soon pulled me out; and when I went down next time I curled my trunk up, so then I was all right."

The other circus animals liked so much to hear Umboo's story of sliding down hill, that they kept asking him questions about it until nearly dinner time. But when the men came in the tent, bringing hay for the horses, elephants and camels, big chunks of meat for the lions and tigers, and dried bread for the monkeys, then all the animals were quiet for a time—at least they made no noise except chewing.

And after their meal they all went to sleep for a little while, those in cages curling up in a corner, and the horses lying down on straw, but the elephants took their sleep standing up, for an elephant, even in the jungle, never lies down except perhaps to roll in water, or a mud-puddle. And the only time they lie down in a circus is when they are doing some trick.

"Now I guess you have slid down hill enough, Umboo," said the elephant's mother to him. "It is all right to have some fun, but there are other things to do in the jungle besides that. You must learn a few things."

"I had to learn things too," said Woo-Uff. "I had to learn how to creep up on fat goats, and knock them over with my big paws. There was an old lion named Boom-Boom, and he and I—"

"Wait a minute! Wait a minute!" called Humpo, the camel, as he was chewing some hay in the circus tent after his dinner. "Is this your story, or Umboo's?"

"Oh, I forgot. I beg your pardon, Umboo!" said the big lion. "Please go on."

So Umboo went on telling his story, speaking of how his mother told him there were other things to do in the jungle besides sliding down hill to splash into the river.

It was some time after this, when Umboo had grown larger and stronger, and two of his tusks or teeth, had grown out of his jaw, sticking far beyond his lips, that his mother said to him:

"Now, Umboo, it is time you learned how to get something to eat for yourself. Up to now I have given you milk, or you have eaten the sweet palm nuts or the tree branches I pulled down for you, or those the other elephants left. Now it is time you learned to do things for yourself. Come with me, Umboo."

"Where are we going?" asked the small elephant. That is he was smaller than his mother, though he was very large along side of a dog or a cat. "Where are we going?"

"Far into the jungle," answered Mrs. Stumptail.

Umboo followed after her, brushing his way through the bushes, pushing aside even those that had thorns on them, for he never felt the sharp pricks through his thick skin, though, as I have told you, some kinds of bugs can bite their way through even this.

Suddenly, as Umboo walked along behind his mother, he began to sniff the air through his trunk.

"What is that good smell?" he asked, in elephant talk, of course. "It smells just like those nice, sweet roots you gave me to eat the other day."

"And that is just what you do smell, Umboo," said his mother. "Near here, in the jungle, grow trees with those sweet roots. If you want to eat some now see if you can find any. In that way you will learn when I am not with you. Hunt around now, and see if you can't smell where the sweet roots grow."

Umboo was hungry and he wanted, very much, to get the roots. So he began sniffing with his trunk close to the ground. When he moved one way the smell was not so strong.

"That means you are moving away from the roots," his mother told him.

"Come over this way."

So Umboo moved the other way, and the smell of the sweet roots grew stronger, just as when you come nearer to a bakery or candy shop.

"Ah! Here they are! Right down under the ground, here!" suddenly cried Umboo, tapping with his trunk on a certain place under a big tree.

"The roots are here, mother," he said. "But how am I going to get them out? I can't eat them if they are under the dirt!"

"How would you think you might get them out?" asked Mrs. Stumptail. "Come, be a smart elephant, Umboo. Use your brains. Elephants are the smartest animals in the world. Think a little and then see what you will do."

So Umboo thought, and then he remembered seeing what the other elephants did when they were hungry, and wanted to dig up tree roots.

"I guess I'll poke away the dirt with my feet," he said.

"Yes, that's a good way to begin," said Mrs. Stumptail.

So Umboo, with his big, broad fore feet, loosened the dirt over the tree roots. They were not down very deep, being the top roots, and not the big heavy ones, buried far down in the earth.

"Ha! Now I can see the roots!" cried the little boy elephant. "They are uncovered, but still I can't lift them up with my trunk, mother. What shall I do next?"

"What are your tusks for?" asked Mrs. Stumptail. "Don't be so silly! Pry up the roots with your tusks!"

So Umboo knelt down and put one of his big long teeth under a root.

Then with a twist of his head he pried the root up from the ground.

"There! See how easy it is!" said his mother.

Then Umboo chewed the sweet root, but he did not swallow the hard, woody part. That would not have been good for him.

"Oh, but this is sweet!" he cried, shutting his eyes as he chewed away. "This is the sweetest root I ever ate."

"And you dug it up yourself! That is best part of it," said his mother. "You have learned to do something for yourself. Now, when you find yourself alone in the jungle, if you should stray away from the rest of the herd, you will know how to get something to eat. You have learned something."

"Is this all I have to learn?" Umboo wanted to know.

"Indeed not!" cried his mother. "There are many more things that you must know. But one thing at a time. A little later I will show you how to pull down a big tree, when there are palm nuts, or sweet branches, growing near the top, which you cannot reach, no matter how you try. Pulling trees down will be the next lesson. But dig up some more roots."

"I will dig some for you," said Umboo.

"Excuse me for not giving you some of the first ones I dug."

"Oh, that's all right," said Mrs. Stumptail. "I wanted you to learn, but you may give me some of the next ones you pry up."

Umboo uncovered more roots, and gave his mother some, and then, as he was moving to another part of the jungle, there suddenly sounded through the forest a loud, shrill cry.

"Quick, Umboo, come with me!" cried his mother. "That is Tusker calling us!"

"What does he want?" asked Umboo.

"He wants to tell us there is danger!" said Umboo's mother. "Hurry!

Come with me back to the rest of the herd!"

CHAPTER V

PICKING NUTS

Not stopping to dig up any more roots, Umboo rushed off through the jungle after his mother, who hurried on ahead. As they crashed along, breaking their way through bushes and knocking down small trees, they heard again the shrill trumpet of Tusker, the oldest and largest elephant of the jungle.

"What is he saying?" asked Umboo of his mother, as he hurried along, now close to her. "What is Tusker saying?"

"He is telling of some kind of danger," said the older elephant. "Just what it is I don't know. But the herd will be moving away very soon, to hide in a dark part of the jungle, and we must go with them."

As Umboo and his mother came out into an open part of the forest, where they had left the other elephants, when Umboo had been led away to be given his root-digging lesson, there was great excitement. Tusker stood on top of a little hill, his trunk high in the air, making all sorts of queer, trumpeting noises.

"We were waiting for you," said Mr. Stumptail to Umboo's mother. "We are going to run away and hide. Tusker is calling you."

"Well, tell him we are here now," said Mrs. Stumptail. "I had to give

Umboo his lesson."

"And I dug up some sweet roots," said the little elephant, "but I didn't have time to bring you any," he told his father.

"Some other time will do," spoke Mr. Stumptail. "Hello, Tusker!" he called through his trunk to the old, big elephant. "Here they are now! Umboo and his mother have come back. We can all go hide in the jungle."

"Why must we hide?" asked Umboo.

"Because Tusker smelled danger," answered Keedah, who was with the other small elephants where they were gathered together, the older ones about them. "He smelled white and black hunters, with guns, and they are coming to shoot us, Tusker says. So he called a warning to all of us."

"I heard it away off where I was digging up roots," said Umboo. "But did Tusker see the hunters with their guns?"

"No, I didn't see them," said Tusker himself, coming down from the hill just then. "But I smelled them, and that is the same thing. The wind was blowing from them to me, and I could smell them very plainly. Come now, elephants! Into the deep, dark part of the jungle, where the hunters can not find us, we will go—far into the jungle."

Then the herd moved off, and Umboo's mother told him, as they hurried along, that an elephant's eyes can not see very far.

"We have not a very sharp sight, like the hawks or the vultures," said Mrs. Stumptail, "so we have to depend on our noses. We can smell things a long way off, and when you are older you will get to know the difference between the sweet roots, under the ground, and the man-smell, which means danger.

"Tusker smelled the man-smell, even though he could not see the white and black hunters, and then he trumpeted through his trunk to tell us all to run away," said Mrs. Stumptail.

Through the jungle crashed the herd of elephants, not going any faster, though, than Umboo and the other small ones could trot along. Though an elephant is very big and heavy he can move swiftly through the forest, and go in places where no horse could travel, for the way would be too rough, and great vines and trees would be strung across the path. Indeed there is no path, the elephants making one for themselves, and when once a herd starts off it can hardly ever be caught by a hunter on foot.

"Do you think any of us will be shot?" asked Umboo, as he shuffled along beside his mother. "How does it feel to be shot?"

"My! But you ask a lot of questions," said Mrs. Stumptail; and I think Umboo was like a lot of boys and girls I know. But then if you don't ask questions how are you ever going to find out anything?

"I can tell you how it feels to be shot," said a middle-aged elephant, who was hurrying along, next to Mr. Stumptail. "It hurts very much, Umboo! It hurts very much, and worse than a whole lot of big bugs biting you at once."

"Were you ever shot?" asked Umboo.

"Indeed I was," answered the elephant, whose name was Bango, called so because he used to bang big trees down with his head. "I was shot twice."

"Tell me about it," said Umboo.

"It was some years ago," went on Bango. "I was with another herd, and we were eating away in the jungle. All at once I heard a noise like a little clap of thunder, and I felt a sharp pain in my head. One of the hard things the hunters shoot in their guns had hit me. Then another struck me in the leg."

"Didn't any of you smell the hunter coming?" asked Mr. Stumptail.

"Didn't you smell him and get out of the way?"

"No," answered Bango, "none of us did. The wind was blowing the wrong way, I guess. But as soon as we heard the gun, and when I gave a blast through my trunk, as I felt myself hurt, then all the herd knew what had happened, and away we rushed, just as we are rushing now. We went very fast."

"Did the hunter get any of you?" asked Umboo.

"Not that time. I was the only one hit," said Bango. "But another time five or six of the herd I was with were killed by hunters."

"What for?" asked Keedah, who was now more friendly with Umboo. "Why did the hunters kill the elephants, Bango?"

"To get their big teeth, or tusks. Our tusks are ivory, you know, and the hunter men, so I have been told, take our teeth to make into round balls, with which they play games, or they use them to put on machines that make tinkle-tinkle sounds."

By this Bango meant pianos, the keys of which used to be made from ivory, though now they are mostly celluloid. And the game men play, with balls made from elephants' tusks, is called billiards.

On and on through the jungle hurried the elephants, until at last

Tusker, who led the way, came to a stop.

"This is far enough," he said. "I do not believe the hunters will find us here. We will rest now."

Indeed it was time to stop, for some of the smaller elephants were quite tired out. Big elephants can hurry through the jungle very fast for as long as twenty hours at a time, stopping, perhaps, only during the very hottest part of the day. And when an elephant is very tired it begins to perspire, or "sweat," over each eye, and two little hollow places there look as though they had been wet with a sponge.

In the cooler part of the shady jungle the elephants rested, some of them pulling down branches from the trees to get at the leaves or tender bark. Umboo began sniffing along the ground with his trunk.

"What are you doing?" asked Keedah.

"I am smelling for sweet roots," was the answer. "My mother showed me how to do it. Do you want me to show you?"

"I learned that long ago," said Keedah.

"Why I can even get palm nuts off a high tree by knocking the tree down. Can you do that? Smelling out earth-roots is nothing!"

"I think it is something," spoke Umboo. "And, when I get a little bigger my mother is going to show me how to pull over, or knock down, a whole tree. But now I am hungry for roots."

So Umboo kept on sniffing at the ground with his trunk. He was feeling quite hungry. Suddenly Keedah cried:

"Ha! I have found some sweet roots! I am going to dig them up!"

"And I have found some, too!" exclaimed Umboo, as through his long nose of a trunk he sniffed the good smell.

Then the two elephant boys dug up the earth with their feet, sort of pawing aside the soft dirt, and with their tusks they pried up the roots, chewing the soft part.

At first the older elephants were uneasy, or worried, for fear that, even though they were in a deep part of the jungle, the hunters might come after them. Tusker and some of the big father-elephants went about, with their trunks high in the air, sniffing, sniffing and sniffing for any smell of danger.

But there seemed to be none. The hunters were left many miles away, and the elephants could rest and eat in peace. For many months after this they roamed about, going from place to place in the jungle as they ate one spot bare of roots and leaves. Sometimes the place where they drank water would dry up, and they would have to move to another river or spring. For an elephant must have plenty of water.

All this while Umboo kept on digging up sweet roots when ever he felt he wanted some, until he could do it almost as well as his mother or father could.

One day, when the elephant boy was traveling through the jungle he looked up and saw, growing on top of a tree, some palm nuts. Elephants are very fond of these, and will go a great way to get them. There are many kinds of palm trees, and on some grow cocoanuts, and on others dates; but the palm nuts the elephants eat are different.

Umboo looked up at the palm nuts growing on the tree in the jungle, and said:

"Oh, how I wish I had some of those."

"Well," said Mrs. Stumptail, "how do you think you can get them?"

"If I were a monkey," said the elephant boy, "I could climb up the tree and pick them off." Umboo had often, in the jungle, seen the monkeys do this.

"But you are not a monkey," said his mother. "Can you reach up with your trunk and pull down the nuts?"

Umboo tried, but his trunk was not long enough.

"I guess the only way to get the nuts is to break down the tree; but how can I do that?" he asked.

"Your head is the strongest part of you," said Mrs. Stumptail. "See if you can knock the tree over."

"Bang!" went Umboo's head against the tree. The tree shook and shivered, and a few nuts were knocked down, but not enough.

"Well," said the elephant boy, as he banged the tree again, "I don't mind doing this for fun, as it doesn't hurt, but the tree doesn't seem to be coming down very fast. And I can't get the nuts until it does. What shall I do, mother?"

"Just think a little harder," said Mrs. Stumptail. "I want you to grow up to be a smart elephant boy, and to do that you must think for yourself. I shall not always be with you. Try and think now how to get the tree down."

"I know!" cried Umboo. "I can pull it over with my trunk!"

He wrapped his long trunk around the tree and began to pull. He had often pulled up small trees and bushes this way, but the palm nut tree was stronger. Though Umboo pulled and pulled, digging his feet hard down into the ground, the tree did not come up.

"Oh, dear!" said the elephant boy. "I don't believe anyone can get this tree down, Mother!"

"Nonsense!" exclaimed Mrs. Stumptail. "Don't be such a baby. Think hard, Umboo! You can easily uproot that tree and get all the nuts you want. Let me see you do it!"

CHAPTER VI

UMBOO IS LOST

Umboo wanted to grow up to be a big, strong smart elephant. He wanted to be like Tusker, the leader of the herd, and he thought if he were as tall, and strong as that mighty fellow he would have no trouble at all in uprooting the tree.

"There must be some way of doing it," said Umboo to himself as he looked up at the palm nuts on top of the tree, and then he glanced at his mother who was watching him. Of course Mrs. Stumptail herself could easily have pulled the tree for Umboo, as it was not very large, but she did not want to do this. Just as your mother wants you to learn to lace your own shoes, or button them, and tie your hair ribbons.

As he stood thinking of what best to do, Umboo scraped with his feet in the dirt around the roots of the tree. Soon he uncovered some of the roots. They were not a kind he liked to eat, but, as he saw the roots laid bare, a new idea came into the head of the elephant boy.

"Ha! I know what I can do!" he said. "I can make the roots loose with my long tusks, and then it will be easy to push the tree over with my head. The roots won't hold it up any more!"

"That's it!" exclaimed his mother. "I was wondering how long it would take you to think of that. And it is better that you should think of it for yourself than that I should tell you. Now you will never forget. So loosen the dirt around the roots, Umboo, and then see what happens."

Kneeling down, Umboo put his tusks under the roots and pried them up, as he used to pry the sweet ones up which he liked to eat. In a little while he had broken many of the big roots. Then he stood up, backed away from the tree, and rushed at it to strike it with his big head which was like a battering-ram.

Once, twice, three times Umboo hit the tree. It shivered and shook, and then, because the roots no longer held it up, over it went with a crash.

"Hurray!" cried Umboo, or what meant the same thing in elephant talk.

"Now I can get the palm nuts!"

"Yes," said his mother. "You have learned something else."

With the tree lying flat on the ground, it was easy for Umboo to reach the palm nuts with his trunk. He pulled them off and ate them, first, though, giving his mother some. For elephants, and other animals, know how to be kind and polite, though of course, they are not so good at it as are you boys and girls.

As Umboo and his mother were eating the palm nuts, along came Keedah.

"Hello!" cried the other elephant boy. "How did you get the palm tree down, Mrs. Stumptail?"

"I did it," said Umboo.

"You?" cried Keedah. "No! You are not strong enough for that!"

"No, I wasn't strong enough to knock this tree over with my head, or pull it down with my trunk, until I loosened the dirt at the roots," said Umboo. "After that it was easy."

"Well, you are getting to be like us bigger boys," said Keedah. "May I have some of the palm nuts, Umboo?"

"Yes," was the answer, for Umboo felt a little proud at what he had done, and, like a real person, he wanted others to know it.

"Did you ever knock down a palm tree?" asked Umboo of Keedah.

"Often," was the answer. "I learned to dig at the roots just as you did. But when it rains you don't have to do that."

"Why not?" Umboo wanted to know.

"Because the rain water makes the dirt soft around the roots, and we don't have to dig it loose with our tusks. Wait until some day when it rains, and you'll see how easy it is to knock over bigger trees than this."

And Umboo found that this was so. About a week after that it rained hard, and to the hot, tired and dusty elephants in the jungle the cooling showers were a delight. The rain soaked into the ground, until it was wet and soft, like a sponge.

Umboo, splashing in a mud puddle, walked away from where he had been standing near his mother.

"Where are you going?" asked Mrs. Stumptail.

"I am going to see if I can do as Keedah said he could do, and knock over a tree without digging at the roots," answered the elephant boy. "The ground is rain-soaked now, and soft."

"Very well," spoke his mother. "You may try it. But don't go too far away. The herd may move on through the jungle, and then you would be lost."

"I'll be careful," promised Umboo.

Off started the elephant boy, splashing through the mud and water. He did not need to wear rubber boots, or take an umbrella. In fact he would not have known what to do with either, though once, in a circus, I saw an elephant with an umbrella. But then I saw one with a hand organ, too, and you'd never see that in the jungle.

But Umboo's big feet were made for walking in mud and water, and his thick skin, though bugs could bite through it at times, did not let any rain leak through to wet him. There was plenty on the outside, however, just as there is outside your rubber coat.

"I'll just go off by myself and knock a great big tree over with my head," thought Umboo. "Then the other elephants will see what I can do. I wonder if it will be easy, on account of the ground being soft from the rain?"

On and on through the jungle wandered Umboo. He was big enough to travel by himself now, though of course he did not want to leave his mother, nor the herd, which was like home to him. He was one of a big family of elephants, some being his sisters, his brothers or his cousins.

All around him, through the forest, Umboo could hear the other elephants crashing about in the wet. They were looking for good things to eat, and none of them went very far away from the others. They wanted to be near where they could hear Tusker sound his trumpet call of danger, if he had to do so.

But Umboo being young, and perhaps rather foolish, thought he could go off as far as he pleased into the jungle.

"I can find my way back again, after I have knocked over a big tree," he thought to himself. "It will be easy."

The elephant boy saw several trees with bunches of palm nuts on them, but none was large enough for him. He wanted to pick out an extra large one; not as big, of course, as his mother or father or Tusker could have butted over, but still one bigger than the other trees he had been used to knocking down.

At last, when he had tramped on quite a distance through the mud and water of the jungle, Umboo saw before him a fine, large palm tree. Growing in the top, so far up that he could not reach any except the very lowest, and littlest, ones, were a number of clusters of palm nuts.

"Ah! That's the tree I'll knock down!" thought Umboo.

He went up to it, and looked at the ground around the roots. It was soft and spongy as he stepped on it, and water oozed out.

"This ought to be easy," said the elephant to himself. "Very easy!"

He put his head against the trunk of the tree and pushed. At first the tree only swayed a little, as though blown by the wind. Then the elephant boy, who was quite strong now, pushed harder and harder. Then he drew back his head and struck the palm tree a hard blow.

And then, all of a sudden, over it went, the roots pulling loose from the soft, wet ground. Over the tree went, falling with a crash!

"Ah ha!" laughed Umboo. "That's the way to do it! Keedah was right! It is very easy to knock over a tree when the ground is soft and muddy. Now for some good nuts to eat."

With his trunk Umboo pulled the palm nuts off the tree and stuffed them into his mouth. An elephant's trunk is to him what your hands are to you children.

After he had eaten as many of the nuts as he wanted (and you may be sure that was quite a number, for elephants have big appetites) Umboo tore off a large branch, with nuts clinging to it and started off through the jungle with it.

"I'll take this back to the herd with me," he thought. "My mother or father may like it. And I can show it to Keedah. He can tell by the size of this branch that the tree I knocked over must be a big one. Then I'll bring him here and show him the tree. I'm almost as big and strong as he is."

So thinking, Umboo went on through the forest. Each tree, leaf and vine was dripping water, for it was still raining hard. Steam arose from the ground, for the earth was hot and the water was warm, as it always is in the jungle.

Perhaps it was this steam, which was like a fog, rising all around him, that puzzled Umboo. And most certainly he was puzzled, for, when he had been walking quite a distance, he suddenly stopped and listened.

"This is strange," he said to himself. "I don't hear any of the other elephants. And I ought to be back with the herd now."

He listened more carefully, flapping his ears which were, by this time, about as large as a baby's bath tub. They were still growing. To and fro Umboo moved his ears, listening first one way and then the other. He could hear the patter of the rain, and the chatter of a monkey now and then, also the fluttering of the big jungle birds, with, every little while, the rustle of a snake. But the elephant boy could not hear the noise made by the other elephants.

"I guess I haven't walked far enough," he said to himself. "I must go along through the jungle some more. But I did not think I came as far as this when I was looking for a tree to knock over."

So, taking a tighter hold of the branch of palm nuts in his trunk, off started Umboo again, splashing through the muddy puddles. He looked this way and that, and he listened every now and then, stopping to do this, for he made so much noise himself, as he hurried along, that he could hear nothing else.

"Well, this is certainly funny!" thought Umboo, when he had stopped and listened about ten times. "I can't hear any other elephants at all. I wonder if they could have gone away and left me?"

Then he knew, that, though the other animals might have gone away and left him, his father and mother would not do this.

"And," thought Umboo, "if there had been any danger from hunters and their guns, Tusker would have sounded his call, and I would have heard that. I guess I haven't gone back far enough."

Then he hurried on again, but, after awhile, when he had listened and could hear nothing of the herd of elephants, and could not see them through the trees, Umboo began to be afraid.

"I guess I must be lost!" he said. "That's it! My mother said it might happen to me, and it has. I'm lost!"

And so he was! Poor Umboo was lost in the jungle, and the rain was coming down harder than ever!

CHAPTER VII

UMBOO AND THE SNAKE

"Weren't you terribly frightened?" asked Chako, the lively monkey, as he swung by his tail from a bar in the top of his circus cage. "Weren't you dreadfully scared, Umboo, when you found out you were lost in the jungle?"

"Indeed I was," answered the elephant boy, who was telling his story to his friends in the big, white tent.

"I was lost once, in the jungle like that," went on the monkey chap, "and all I had to eat was a cocoanut. And I—"

"Wait a minute! Wait a minute!" cried Humpo the camel. "Are we listening to your story, Chako, or to Umboo's?"

"Oh, that's so! I forgot!" exclaimed Chako. "Go on, Umboo. I won't talk any more."

"Well, I won't either—at least for a while," said Umboo. "For here come the keepers with our dinners. Let's eat instead of talking."

And surely enough, into the circus tent came the men with the food for the animals—hay for the elephants, meat for the lions and tigers, and dried bread and peanuts for the monkeys.

Then after a sleep, which most animals take about as soon as they have eaten, it was time for the circus to begin. Into the tent where the jungle folk were kept, came the boys and girls, with their fathers and mothers, or uncles, aunts and cousins.

"Oh, look at the big elephant!" cried one boy. "I'm going to give him some peanuts!" and he stopped in front of Umboo.

"No, don't!" cried a little girl who was with the boy. "He might bite you."

"Pooh! He can't!" said the boy. "He can only reach me with his long nose of a trunk, and there aren't any teeth in that. His teeth are in his mouth, farther up."

"Well, he's got a pinching thing on the end of his trunk," spoke the little girl, "and he can nip you."

"I don't guess he will," went on the boy. "Anyhow I'd like to give him some peanuts."

"And I'd like to have them," said Umboo, in elephant talk, of course, which the other animals could understand, but which was not known to the little boy and girl, nor to the other children in the circus tent.

Then the little boy grew brave, and held out a bag, partly filled with peanuts, to Umboo, who took them in his trunk, and chewed them up, first, though, taking them out of the bag, for he did not like to chew paper.

"I wish I could ride on the elephant's back!" said the little boy.

"Children do ride on the backs of elephants in India, the country where you and I came from, don't they, Umboo?" asked Snarlie, the tiger, when the children had passed on to the tent where the performers were to do their circus tricks.

"Oh, yes, many a ride I have given children in India," said Umboo.

"But that was after I was caught in the jungle trap and tamed."

"Tell us about that!" begged Chako.

"All in good time! All in good time," said the big elephant, in a sort of drowsy voice, for he had hardly slept through all his nap that day, before the circus crowds came in. "I have yet to tell you how I was lost, and how I got back to the rest of the herd. But seeing the children remind me of the days in India," added Umboo.

"And it reminded me also," spoke Snarlie. "Well do I recall how little Princess Toto rode on the back of a great elephant like yourself, Umboo, and how it was then I first saw her. Afterward I went to live with her, and there was a palace, with a fountain in it where the water sparkled in the sun."

"What's a palace?" asked Chako, the monkey. "Is it something good to eat, like a cocoanut?"

"Indeed it is not," said Snarlie. "A palace is a big house, like this circus tent, only it is made of stone. Princess Toto and I lived there, but now I live in a circus, and I shall never see Toto again! I liked her very much."

"I like children, too," said Woo-Uff, the lion, in his deep, rumbly voice. "Once a little African boy named Gur was kind to me, and gave me a drink of water when I was caught in the net. He was a good boy."

"Did he ride on an elephant's back?" asked Snarlie.

"I never saw him do that," answered the lion, "though he may have. But the elephants of Africa, where I came from, are wilder, larger and more fierce than those of India, where our friend Umboo used to live. People hardly ever ride on an African elephant's back."

"Well, let us hear more of Umboo's story," suggested Humpo, the camel.

"It seems to me everyone is talking but him."

"That's so," spoke Horni, the rhinoceros. "Please go on, Umboo. Tell us about how you were lost in the jungle."

So the big circus elephant, slowly swaying to and fro, and gently clanking his chains, told more of his jungle story.

When he looked all around among the trees, which were dripping water from the heavy rain, and when he could not see any of the other elephants, Umboo felt very badly indeed. For animals, even those who live in the jungle, get lonesome, the same as you boys and girls do when you go away from home.

"Well, if I am lost," thought Umboo to himself, as he held the branch of palm nuts, "I must see if I can not find the way home." For though elephants have no real home, traveling as they do to and fro in the jungle so much, Umboo called "home" the place where he had last seen his mother and the rest of the herd.

Since Umboo could not see a long way through the trees, as he might have done if he had eyes as sharp and bright as a big vulture bird, he had to do what most elephants do—smell. So he raised his trunk in the air, dropping the palm branch to the ground, and sniffed as hard as he could. He wanted to smell the elephant smell—the odor that would come from the herd of the big animals who were somewhere in the jungle eating leaves and bark.

But Umboo could not smell them. Nor could he smell any danger, and he was glad of that.

All the smells that came to him were those of the jungle—the soft mud smell, the odor of wet, green leaves and the smell of the falling rain. All those smells Umboo knew and loved. But he could not smell the other elephants, and if he could have done so he would have known which way to walk to get to them.

Slowly he turned himself around, so as to smell each way the wind blew, toward him and from him. But it was of no use. No elephant smell came to him.

"I guess I am too far away," thought the elephant boy to himself. "I must walk on farther. Then I'll come to where my mother is. I wish I had not gone away from her."

Picking up the palm branch again, with the sweet nuts still fast to it, Umboo started off once more through the mud and water. The rain came down harder than ever, but he did not mind that. It washed his skin of the dried mud and dust that had been on it some time, and when it rained the bugs did not bite so much. Also the rain was not cold, for it was pleasant and warm in the jungle. Only it was lonesome to the elephant boy, who, never before, had been so long away from his mother.

On he tramped, splashing this way and that through the puddles, wading through little brooks and, once, even swimming over a small river, for, by this time Umboo was as good a swimmer as the other elephants.

"But I don't remember swimming that river before," said Umboo to himself, as he crawled out on the farther bank, with the branch of palm nuts held high in his trunk. "Surely I must have come the wrong way. I am worse lost than ever!"

And so Umboo was. But there was no help for it. He must keep on, and he hoped, before it grew dark, that he would find the herd, and his mother with it.

After he had swum across the river Umboo pushed on through the jungle for a mile or more. All at once he heard, off to one side, something crashing through the bushes much as he was doing.

"Ha! Perhaps that is another elephant!" thought Umboo. "Maybe it is my mother or my father, or perhaps Old Tusker coming to look for me. I shall be glad of that!

"Hello there!" cried Umboo in elephant talk. "Is that you, Mother?

Here I am, over here!"

The crashing of the bushes stopped, and a loud voice said:

"No, I am not your mother. What is the matter with you, elephant boy?" and out of the jungle came stalking a big rhinoceros. On his head, close to the end of his nose, grew a long, sharp horn. At first Umboo was afraid of this horn, but the rhinoceros did not seem to be cross, and the elephant boy went closer to him.

"The matter with me," said Umboo, "is that I am lost. I went out in

the jungle, away from where our herd of elephants was feeding, and now

I can't find my way back again. Can you tell me where my mother is,

Mr. Rhino?"

"I am sorry to say that I can not," answered the rhinoceros, scratching his leg with his horn. "But why did you go away from the herd?"

"I wanted to go out in the jungle and knock over a big tree," said Umboo. "Keedah, one of the boys in the herd, said it was easy to do when the ground was soft from the rain."

"And did you do it?" asked the rhinoceros.

"Yes," answered Umboo, "I did. This branch of palm nuts is from the tree I knocked over with my head. I'd give you some, only I am saving them for my mother."

"Oh, that's all right; thank you," said the other jungle beast. "I don't care much for palm nuts anyhow, and I'd rather you would save them for your mother."

"Do you know where my mother is?" asked Umboo eagerly.

"I am sorry to say I do not," was the reply. "I have been wandering about the jungle myself, looking for a rhinoceros friend of mine, but I haven't found him."

"Did you see a herd of elephants?" asked Umboo eagerly.

"No, I didn't exactly see them," answered Mr. Rhino, "but about two showers ago I heard a big noise in the jungle back of me, and perhaps that was the elephant herd."

Mr. Rhino said "two showers ago," instead of "two hours," you see, because the jungle animals have no clocks or watches, and they tell time by the sun, or by the number of rain-showers in a day. And Umboo knew that very well, so he knew about how long ago it was that the rhinoceros had heard the loud sounds of which he spoke.

"Oh, so you heard the elephants, did you?" exclaimed Umboo. "I am glad of that. Now I'll hurry off and find them. Thank you for telling me."

"Oh, that's all right," politely answered the rhinoceros. "I hope you find your mother and other friends. Good-bye!"

He wiggled his horn at Umboo, who waved his trunk with the palm tree branch in it, and once more, off through the jungle started the elephant boy.

On and on he went. But either he did not go the right way, or two showers ago was longer than either he or the rhinoceros thought, for Umboo did not even smell the other elephants, much less see them or hear them.

"Oh, dear!" thought Umboo again. "I'm surely lost as bad as before!

What shall I do?"

He stood and looked about him in the dripping wet jungle. He felt hungry, but he did not like to eat the palm nuts he was saving for his mother, so he chewed some leaves from a tree, and nibbled a bit of bark. But neither was as good as the palm nuts would have been.

Then, as Umboo stood there, he suddenly heard a loud, hissing noise. It seemed to come from right under his feet, and, looking down, he saw a large snake.

Now all jungle animals are afraid of snakes for the serpents can bite and poison at the same time. So though a snake may not be very strong, he can kill by poison some of the strongest beasts. Thus it was that Umboo, who would have fought even a tiger, was afraid of the snake.

"Ah, ha! You would nip me, would you?" cried the elephant, as he raised his big foot to crush the snake before it had a chance to bite and poison him.

CHAPTER VIII

UMBOO FINDS HIS MOTHER

"Did the snake bite you?" asked Chako, the funny monkey chap, who was hanging by his tail, upside down, listening to the story told by Umboo. "Did the snake bite you?"

"Oh, can't you keep quiet?" asked Woo-Uff, the lion, in his deep, rumbly voice. "Let Umboo alone! He'll tell us what happened."

"Oh, I beg your pardon," said Chako. "I was so anxious that I could hardly wait to hear. We monkeys are very much afraid of snakes, you know."

"So I have heard," said Woo-Uff. "Please go on, Umboo."

So Umboo told the rest of his story.

In the jungle he stood, with one foot raised, ready to crush the big snake.

"Please do not step on me!" hissed the snake, for that was his way of talking. "Please do not put your big foot on me, elephant boy!"

"But I am afraid you will bite me," said Umboo.

"No, I'll not do that," answered the snake. "I do sometimes bite, when I am hungry, but I am not hungry now. Besides, you are quite too big to bite."

"Oh, ho, if you feel that way about it, all right," said Umboo, and he put his foot down, but not on the snake. "There are much larger elephants though, than I am. I wish I could see some of them now. Tell me," he asked the hissing serpent, "did you see anything of the elephant herd on your travels through the jungle?"

"No, not exactly," the snake made answer. "But, as you were kind enough not to step on me, I will do you a favor. I will show you the way through the jungle to where the other elephants are.

"Can you do it?" asked Umboo.

"Surely," replied the snake. "We serpents are the wisest of all creatures, not even excepting you big elephants. For we have to stay so low down on the ground that we would easily be stepped on and killed by other beasts, if we were not wise enough to keep out of the way. So, though I have not seen your mother, or the elephant herd, I can find them for you."

"How did you know I was looking for my mother?" asked Umboo. "I did not tell you that."

"No, but you told the rhinoceros," said the snake.

"Ha! Then you must have very good ears, Mrs. Snake, to have heard that, for it was a long way from here," said Umboo. "You must have very good ears indeed, though they are not as large as mine. In fact I can not see them at all."

"Never mind about my ears," said the snake. "I told you we serpents were very wise. We know many things. And now, if you please, follow me and I will show you the way through the jungle to where your mother is, and the rest of the herd. But as I have to crawl along on the ground, please be careful not to step on me. We snakes do not like to be stepped on."

"I'll be careful," promised Umboo.

Then the snake glided, or crawled, along through the jungle, and Umboo, watching which way she went, followed, carrying in his trunk the branch of palm nuts for his mother.

On and on went the snake, now and then stopping to coil and raise her head above the ground so she might listen. The water drops glistened on her shiny scales, and she was very beautiful in color, though she was so dangerous and deadly.

"What are you stopping for?" asked Umboo at one time.

"I am trying to listen to hear the tramp of the herd of elephants," the snake answered. "Do not make any noise."

So Umboo stood still, and was very quiet, but he could hear nothing. However, the snake must have heard, for she uncoiled herself and started off another way, saying:

"Follow me, Umboo."

"How did you know my name was Umboo?" asked the elephant boy. "I did not tell you that."

"We serpents are wise, and know many things," was the answer, and

Umboo began to believe that.

"It is a good thing I met her," he said to himself, as he followed the glistening snake through the jungle. "I am glad I did not step on her as I was first going to do."

On and on through the jungle went Umboo, following the guiding snake, whose glistening scales and bright colors he could easily see amid the green leaves and bushes. At last the snake came to a stop and once more coiled and reared up her head.

"Make no noise, big elephant boy!" she hissed.

Umboo stood still and was very quiet.

"Ha! I thought so!" said the snake. "Go over that way," and she pointed with her head. "Walk about a mile, straight along, and you will come to your mother and the herd of elephants."

"How do you know?" asked Umboo.

"Because I can hear them," answered the snake. "I can hear the tramping of their big feet. I can hear them trumpeting through their long noses of trunks, and I can hear them tearing down the tree branches and stripping off the bark. That is how I know.

"I would go closer, and take you nearer to them, but some of them might step on me, without finding out first, that I would do them no harm. But you can easily find your way from here. Keep straight on," said the snake.

"Thank you, I will," answered Umboo. "I would give you some of these palm nuts, only I am saving them for my mother."

"Thank you," said the snake. "But I do not eat palm nuts. Take them on to your mother, elephant boy."

Then the snake glided away through the jungle, and, watching the end of her tail vanish under a bush, Umboo started off by himself. He had not heard the sounds spoken of by the serpent, but he knew the noises were such as a herd of elephants would make.

"She must have good ears, to hear what she heard," thought the elephant boy. "And yet her ears were not as large as mine."

So, flapping his own big ears, and wishing he could hear with them as well as the snake could with her small ones, Umboo stalked on through the jungle in the way she had told him to go.

It was not very long before he heard a crashing sound. Then he lifted his trunk, still holding the palm branch, and he sniffed and snuffed. And then, to the long, rubbery nose of the elephant boy, came the wild smell of other jungle animals.

"Ah! Now I smell the herd!" he cried. "Now I am not lost any more!

Hurray!"

Of course when an elephant says "Hurray" it is different than the way you boys and girls say it. But it means the same thing.

On hurried Umboo. The crashing noises sounded more plainly now, and the elephant smell became stronger. Then, as he burst his way through the bushes, Umboo saw the other elephants standing together in a little clearing in the jungle, and Umboo's mother seemed to be talking to them.

"Ha!" suddenly cried Keedah, the larger elephant boy, as he saw the lost one. "Here he comes now! Here is Umboo!"

Mrs. Stumptail swung around and started toward him.

"Where in the world have you been?" she asked. "Why, Umboo! I have been so worried about you, and so has your father! We were just going out into the jungle to look for you."

"That's what we were," said Tusker. "And hard work it would have been with night coming on. We want to travel to a new place, too, and looking for you would have held us back. What do you mean by going off by yourself this way?"

"I went to see if I could knock over a big palm tree when the ground was soft from rain," said Umboo.

"And did you do it?" asked Mr. Stumptail.

"I did," answered Umboo. "I knocked over a big tree. It was easy, and here is a branch of it for you, and it has some nuts on," and he handed his mother the one he had brought with him all the way through the jungle.

"Oh, thank you!" said Mrs. Stumptail. "You are a very good boy, Umboo, and I shall like these nuts very much. But why did you stay away so long?"

"I was lost," answered the elephant chap. "I could not find my way back after I knocked over the tree. I met a rhinoceros, but he could not tell me where you were. Then I met a kind snake, and she showed me how to find you."

"Well, don't get lost again," said Umboo's mother. "We are glad you have come back, for, as Tusker says, we are about to travel on, and we did not want to leave you behind. So get ready now, we are going to a new part of the jungle."

A little later the herd started off, and Umboo walked with some of the other young elephants, or calves, as they are called. He told them the different things that happened to him when he was lost in the jungle.

On and on went the herd of elephants. They traveled nearly all night, and the next day they stopped to rest, for the sun was too hot for even such big, strong beasts.

Umboo and the others were feeding in a quiet part of the forest, when suddenly Tusker, who was always on the watch, no matter whether he was eating or not, gave a loud trumpet call.

"Ha! That means danger!" thought Umboo, who, by this time knew the meaning of the different calls. "I wonder what it can be?"

CHAPTER IX

TO THE SALT SPRING

Quickly, as the other elephants in the jungle heard the trumpet call of Tusker, they ran in from the different trees, where they were pulling off leaves or stripping bark, and gathered around the big leader. Tusker stood with upraised trunk, his eyes flashing in the sun.

"What is it?" asked Mr. Stumptail, and some of the others. "What is the matter now?"

"I smell danger," cried Tusker. "I smell the man-smell, and that always means danger to us. There are hunters coming — either black or white — and they will have guns or bows and arrows to shoot us. We are near danger and we must go far away. Come, elephants — away!"

Tusker raised his trunk again, and took a long breath through it. He was smelling to see in which direction the danger of the man-smell lay, and he would turn aside from that.

"The smell comes from the South," he said to the other elephants. "We must march to the North! Come!"

So he led the way through the jungle, Umboo and the other elephants following. As yet only a few of the others had smelled the danger-smell, and none of them heard any noise made by the hunters, if they were coming to shoot their guns or bows and arrows. But they all knew that Tusker was a wise elephant, and would lead them out of trouble. So they followed him.

On and on through the jungle crashed the big animals. They did not stop when trees and bushes got in their way, but broke them down, and stepped on them. A rush of elephants through the jungle to get away from danger is almost as hard to stop as a runaway locomotive and train of cars.

"Can you keep up with us?" asked Umboo's mother of him as he trotted along beside her. "Are we going too fast for you?"

"Oh, no. I can go quite fast now," said the elephant boy, and he really could, for he had grown much in the last few months. Plenty of palm nuts and the bark and leaves of the jungle trees had made him taller and stronger, and his legs were better fitted for running.

Still Tusker was a wise old elephant, and he knew, even in running from danger, that it was not well to go so fast that the smaller animals in the herd could not keep up. If he did that they would fall behind, and be caught or killed. So, every now and then the old elephant leader stopped a bit, and looked back. If he saw any of the boys or girls lagging, or going slow, he would stop for them to rest a little.

Still, even with rests now and then, the herd went on very fast, crashing through the jungle, to get away from the danger. At last Tusker stopped, and said:

"Well, I think we have come far enough. We are beyond the reach of the hunters now. We can stop and eat and sleep in peace."

So the elephants stopped. You see, now, why it was they had no regular homes. They have to move so often, either to go to new places in the jungle to find food, or to run from danger, so that a cave, such as lions or tigers have, or a nest, such as birds live in, would be of no use to elephants. They must live in the open, ready to hurry on for many miles at a moment's notice.

Tusker, and some of the older and wiser beasts, listened as well as they could, flapping their big ears slowly to and fro. They also smelled the air with their trunks. And, as there was no sign of danger, they felt that it would be safe to take a long rest.

They were hungry; for running, or exercise, gives elephants appetites just as it does you boys and girls. And some of the smaller elephants were sleepy. For, though they do not lie down to rest, elephants must sleep, as do other beasts, although they do it standing up. That night the herd remained quietly in the new spot in the jungle whither Tusker had led them. Some of them ate and some of them slept, and when morning came they went to a river of water; and each one took a long drink. Some of them swam about, and it was now that Umboo and the young elephants had some fun.

For you know that jungle beasts—even the largest of them—like to play and have fun. You have seen kittens at play, and puppy dogs; and little lions and tigers, as well as the smaller elephants, like to do the same thing—have fun.

Umboo was standing on the bank of the river, having just been in for a swim, when Batu, another elephant boy, came up to him.

"Do you want to have some fun?" asked Batu.

"Yes," answered Umboo. "What doing?"

"Do you see Keedah over there, scraping his toe nails on a big stone?" asked Batu, for sometimes the toe nails of elephants grow too long and too rough, and have to be worn down. Keedah was doing this to his.

"Yes, I see him," answered Umboo. "What about him?"

"This," answered Batu, with a chuckling laugh that made him shake all over, for he was quite fat. "We will go up to him, as he stands with his back to the water, and while I am talking to him, and asking if his toe nails hurt, you can give him a push and knock him into the river."

"Oh, yes, we'll do that. It will be fun!" laughed Umboo.

For he knew that it would not hurt Keedah to splash into the water, and the elephant boys and girls used often to play that trick on one another, just as you children, perhaps, do at the seashore.

So up to the elephant boy, who was scraping his toe nails on a stone, slyly went Umboo and Batu. And Batu said:

"Ah, Keedah! Do your toes hurt you very much?"

"Oh, no, not so very much," was the answer. "I am getting to be a big elephant now, and I do not mind a little hurt."

"Ha! Then maybe you won't mind this!" suddenly cried Umboo with a laugh, as he quietly went up close to Keedah, and, butting him with his head, as a goat butts, knocked him down the bank into the river.

"Oh! Ugh! Blurg! Splub!" cried Keedah, as he splattered about in the water. "What are you doing that for?"

"Oh, just to have some fun," answered Umboo and Batu, laughing as they ran off.

"Well, I'll show you some more fun!" cried Keedah, as he scrambled up the river bank, and ran after the other two elephant boys, his trunk raised high in the air.

Umboo and Batu ran as fast as they could, of course, and Keedah raced after them. Finally he caught them, and struck them with his trunk. But it was all in fun, and no one minded it. Then, a little later, when Umboo was standing near the river, Keedah came up behind him and knocked him into the water.

"Now we are even!" laughed Keedah as he ran away.

"I don't mind!" said Umboo. "I was going in for another swim, anyhow.

I like to be wet."

So he splashed about in the water and had fun, as did the other elephant boys and girls, and the larger elephants watched them, and let the water soak into their own tough hides.

For about a week the herd of elephants stayed near the jungle river. It was a good place for them. Many palm trees grew about, and there were plenty of other things to eat. There was water to drink and bathe in, and shade to rest in when the sun beat down too hot on the jungle. So the elephants liked it there.

But one day when Umboo and Batu were thinking up another fun-trick to play on Keedah, suddenly the trumpet call of Tusker was heard again.

"More danger!" exclaimed Umboo. "I wonder what it is this time?"

"Let us go ask," suggested Batu. "The others are getting ready to leave. They are closing in. Perhaps we have to run away again."

And that is just what the elephants had to do.

"It is the hunters once more!" cried Tusker. "I smell the man-smell! The danger-smell comes down to me on the wind. We must hurry on. Once more the hunters are after us!" and he trumpeted loudly on his trunk, to call in from the farthest parts of the forest the elephants who might have wandered away for food.

Soon the herd was on the march again. Swiftly they went through the jungle, breaking down small trees and big bushes. They stopped not for thorns, nor anything else in the path. On and on they went, crashing along—anywhere to get away from the hunters with their guns and arrows.

"Are these the same hunters from whom we ran before?" asked Umboo of his mother, as he trotted along beside her.

"I do not know," she answered. "It may be that they are."

For many miles Tusker led his elephant friends through the jungle.

Then suddenly he stopped and gave a loud trumpet call.

"Does that mean it is all right, and that we can stop to rest?" asked

Umboo.

"I do not think so," said Mr. Stumptail. "That still is Tusker's danger call. Perhaps there are hunters ahead of us, as well as behind."

Tusker stopped, and around him gathered the other elephants.

"What is the matter?" asked Umboo.

"See, boy," answered the old elephant. "There is a fence of big trees ahead. We can not get through that. It is right across our path," and with his trunk he pointed to where there was, indeed, a high fence made of trees, cut down and set closely in the earth and so strong that even the biggest elephant would have had hard work to knock them down.

"Well, if we can't go that way we can go another," said Tusker.

So he turned about, and walked off another way, the other elephants following him.

"Who put the fence there, Mother?" asked Umboo.

"I do not know," answered Mrs. Stumptail. "Perhaps the hunters did, so we could not get into their gardens and eat the corn and other things that grow there. Very good things grow in the gardens which the white and black men plant, and, more than once in the night, I have broken in and eaten them. But it is dangerous, and Tusker does not want to lead us into danger. We will keep away from the fence."

Now, though the elephants did not know it, this fence was not built to keep elephants out of a garden. There were no gardens in that part of the jungle. The fence was put up by hunters on purpose to turn the elephants back, and soon you shall hear why this was done.

"Are we in danger now?" asked Umboo of his father as they hurried along, close beside Tusker.

"No, I think we are all right now," said the oldest, wisest and largest elephant of the herd. "I am going to lead you to the salt springs, where we can taste the salt of the earth. One way is as good as another, and if the fence stops us on one path we will go a new way. We are going to the salt springs."

Every year the herds of elephants in India come down to eat salt, for they need it to keep them well, as horses and cows do on the farm. And the elephant hunters know this too, and so they get ready to capture the wild elephants when they come down each season to get the salt.

The herd was not going so fast now. Tusker felt that they were well away from the hunters, and, though seeing the fence at first scared him a little, he now thought everything was all right.

"We will have good times when we get to the salt springs," said Tusker to the other elephants. "There we can rest, and the hunters will not shoot us."

"Yes, I am hungry for some salt," said Mrs. Stumptail, for she had been to the springs before, and so had many of the older animals.

Along marched Tusker at the head of the herd, and after him came the others. They, too, were hungry for salt, and Umboo was quite anxious to taste some, for he had had very little, as yet. But he liked it very much, and was anxious for more.

But an hour or so later, when traveling along toward where the salt springs bubbled up in the jungle, Tusker suddenly stopped again. Once more he gave the danger signal through his trunk.

"What is the matter now?" asked Mr. Stumptail. "More trouble?"

"Another fence!" cried the old elephant. "The jungle is full of strong fences! We can not go this way, either!"

"What can we do?" asked Umboo. "There is a fence behind us, and now one in front of us. What can we do?"

"Let me think a minute," said Tusker. "I fear there is danger on both sides of us."

CHAPTER X

IN A TRAP

All the other elephants waited while Tusker stood there, swaying to and fro in the jungle thinking. Some people say animals do not think, but I believe they do. At least it is thinking to them, though it may not seem so to us.

"Well, are we going to stay here all day?" asked a young elephant, who was crowded in among the others at the back of the herd. "I want to get to some place where I can have palm nuts to eat. I am hungry. Let's go on!"

"Be quiet!" called Umboo's father to this elephant. "Don't you see that Tusker is trying to think, and find the best way out of danger for us. Wait a bit."

So the elephants waited, and finally Tusker with a shake of his big ears, said:

"I never knew anything like this before. Always when we have come to the salt springs the way has been clear. There have been no man-made fences to stop us. But, since they are here it must be that it is not meant for us to go where the fences are. Very well. I know how to get to the salt springs without going near these things across our paths. We can go straight ahead, between the two fences!"

And that was just what the hunters, who had put up the fences in the jungle wanted. They wanted the elephants to go along between them, for, at the places where the fences came to an end, was a strong stockade, or trap, to catch the wild elephants.

Umboo, and none of the other elephants knew this at the time, but they learned it later, to their sorrow, some of them. When hunters in the Indian jungle wish to capture a lot of wild elephants, to work for them, or to be turned into trick elephants for the circus, the hunters do this.

First they find the place where, each year, the wild elephants come down from the hills, or out of the jungle, to taste the salt. For, as I told you, elephants must have salt once in a while, just as horses, cows and sheep on the farm need it. The elephants will travel a long way, and brave many dangers, to get salt.

Knowing this the hunters build long fences on each side of the road leading down from the hills to the salt spring. When the elephants crash their way through the jungle, on their way to the salt, they come to one of the fences. This turns them aside, and they go along until they come to another.

Then, just as did Tusker, and his friend Umboo and the other elephants, being between two strong fences, there is only one other thing to do. They can go between them toward the salt spring, or away from it. But, as they want salt very much, the big animals tramp along the two miles of fence toward the salty place, and, knowing the elephants will do this, the hunters are ready for them. Now I shall tell you what happened.

For a few minutes longer Tusker stood swaying in the jungle. He was trying to think what was the best thing for him to do, for he was the leader of the herd, and they would all do as he did, just as a flock of sheep will follow the old ram, even on the dangerous railroad track sometimes.

"Come!" trumpeted Tusker through his trunk, "we will go between the two fences to the salt springs."

"Is the salt good, Mother?" asked Umboo, for he had only had a little in his life, and as I told you, hardly remembered it.

"Very good, indeed," said Mrs. Stumptail. "You shall soon see and taste for yourself."

So along through the jungle, half way between the two lines of fence, went the elephants, little and big. They had not gone very far before, all of a sudden, Tusker stopped and raised his trunk in the air.

"Be careful!" he cried. "I smell danger! I smell the man smell! Oh, elephants, I fear something is going to happen."

And something did happen.

From behind the herd of elephants, and from both sides of them, came a terrible noise. It was as though a hundred thunderbolts had been shot off at once, and a terrible clapping sound was heard, as if the wings of great birds were flapping.

These noises were made by hunters up in the trees on each side of, and behind, the elephants. The hunters fired their guns, making the noise like small thunder bolts and other black men banged pieces of dry wood together, making the clapping sound.

The elephants were very much frightened. Never before had they heard anything like this.

"Oh, what is it?" cried Umboo, keeping close to his mother. "What is it all about. Does the salt spring make that noise?"

"No, it isn't that," said Mrs. Stumptail. "That must be the danger of which Tusker spoke. Be quiet and listen to what he is saying."

The old elephant leader had to trumpet through his trunk as loudly as he could to be heard above the noise of the guns and clappers.

"There is danger, O Elephants!" cried Tusker. "The man-smell is all around us, and the terrible noises are behind, and on both sides of us. There is only one place that is quiet, and that is straight ahead. We must go that way! Forward!"

And straight ahead rushed the elephants, toward the place where there was no noise. As they went on Mr. Stumptail looked to either side and saw where the two lines of fence came together into a place like a big ring, and the ring also had a fence around it.

"Look, Tusker!" cried Umboo's father. "Is it all right to go there where the fence is?"

"It is the only place to go to get away from the hunters," said Tusker. "They are behind us and on both sides. Only ahead of us is there none. We must go that way!"

And this is just what the hunters wanted. They made no noise in front of the elephants on purpose so they would rush that way. For, in that direction, was the strongly fenced-in stockade, or trap, with long barriers on each side leading to it.

To the elephants, who were frightened by the shooting and clapping noises behind, and on both sides of them, the silence in front of them seemed just what they wanted. Toward it they ran, not knowing that the trap was waiting for them.

Into it they rushed, the noise behind them sounding louder and louder now, with more guns shooting and more clappers clapping. Into the quiet of the stockade rushed Tusker, Mr. and Mrs. Stumptail, Umboo, Keedah and all the others.

And then, when they were safely in the trap, a great big door of logs, as strong as the fence of trees of which the stockade was built, fell with a bang behind them, shutting the elephants in. Then the shooting and clapping stopped.

For a moment it was quiet in the jungle, the only sound being the wind blowing in the trees, or the rubbing of the rough-skinned elephants' bodies, one against the other, making a queer, shuffling noise. The big animals crowded together in the middle of the stockade trap, and waited for what would happen next.

"Is this the salt spring, Mother?" asked Umboo.

"No," she sadly answered. "It is not. This is dreadful!"

"What has happened?" asked Umboo. "And why do Tusker and the other big elephants look so scared?"

"Because we are caught in a trap," answered the boy elephant's mother.

"I have heard tell of these places, but I was never in one before."

"Can't we get out?" Umboo wanted to know.

"Tusker will try, and so will your father," said Mrs. Stumptail. "All the strong elephants will try to break out. Perhaps it will be all right yet. Listen, Tusker is going to speak."

Tusker, the big bull, raised his trunk and said:

"O, Elephants! I am sorry, but I seem to have led you into a trap. I did not know it was here. I tried to lead you away from the man-smell and away from the danger, but I have led you into worse. Now I will try to get you out. I see what has happened. The hunters made their fences in the jungle so we could only come this way — this way into the trap. But we shall break out!

"Come over here by me, Mr. Stumptail, and you too, Mr. One Tusk, and you also, Bumper Head. Come, we will rush at the fence of this trap and batter it down. In that way we can get out. We shall fool these hunters yet. Come, we will batter down the fence and once more we will be in our jungle!"

"Yes, we will knock down the fence!" cried the other big elephants through their trunks. And they made such a rumble, and struck the ground so heavily with their great feet, that the earth trembled.

CHAPTER XI

UMBOO GOES TO SCHOOL

"What is going to happen now?" asked Umboo the big elephant boy of his mother, as the great creatures stood huddled together in the middle of the stockade, or trap. "What is going to happen now?"

"Wait and see," advised Mrs. Stumptail, and she was much worried.

I have called Umboo a "big" elephant boy, for he was small no longer. He had grown fast since I began telling you about him as a baby drinking milk, and now, though of course he was not as large as his mother or father, nor as strong as Tusker, I must not call him "little" any more.

"Come, Elephant brothers!" cried Tusker. "We will break down the trap fence, and then we shall be free to go out into our jungle again."

But it was not so easy to do this as it was to say it. The men who had built the fences and trap well know that the elephants would try to get out, and the stockade had been made very strong.

Besides this there had been dug, inside the trap, and close to where the heavy tree-stakes had been driven into the ground, a ditch, or trench. There was no water in this ditch but on account of the trench the elephants could not get near enough the inside of the fence to strike it with their heads. If they had done so they would have gotten their front feet into the dug-out place, and, perhaps, would have fallen over and hurt themselves.

So when Tusker and the others hoped to knock the fence down by hitting, or butting, it with their heads, they found they could not, as the ditch stopped them. They could only just reach the fence by stretching out their trunks; they could not bang it with their big heads as they wanted to.

"Can't we ever get out of the trap?" asked Umboo of his mother when Tusker and the others had found they could not knock down the stockade fence. "Can't we ever get out?"

"And did you ever get out?" eagerly asked Snarlie, the tiger, who, with the other circus animals, listened to Umboo's story. "Did you ever get out of the trap, Umboo?"

"Tell us about that part!" begged Woo-Uff, the lion. "Once I was caught in a trap, but it was made of a net, with ropes of bark. It was then that Gur, the kind boy, gave me a drink of water."

"And I was in a trap also," spoke Snarlie, the striped tiger. "I fell into a deep pit. It was almost like your trap, Umboo, except that the sides were of dirt, and the pit was very deep. I could not jump out. But after a while I did not mind being caught, for I was taken care of by Princess Toto."

"Let us hear how Umboo got out of the trap," said Chako, the monkey.

"How do you know he got out?" asked Humpo, the camel.

"Isn't he here with us now?" asked Chako, who was a very smart monkey. "And if he hadn't got out of the trap he wouldn't be here. Anybody knows that!"

"Oh, yes; that's so," said Humpo, who did not think much, being quite content to eat hay, and let others do most of the talking. "But, all the same," went on the humpy creature, "I should like to hear how Umboo did get out of the trap."

"I'll tell you," said the elephant boy, and he went on with his story.

When the big elephants found, because of the ditch, that they could not get near enough the stockade fence to knock it down with their big heads, they became very wild. They raised their trunks and made loud trumpet sounds through them. They beat the earth with their feet until the ground trembled, and some of them rushed at the gate, which had fallen shut behind them, as they hurried into the trap to get away from the noise.

But the gate, which had no ditch in front of it, was the strongest part of the trap, and the elephants could not batter it down, try as they did. Tusker and the others banged into it, but the gate held firmly.

"Well, if we can't get out, what are we going to do?" asked Umboo of his mother.

"We shall have to stay here until the hunter-men come, I suppose," answered Mrs. Stumptail.

"Will they shoot us?" asked Umboo.

"I hope not," his mother said.

But Umboo need not have been afraid of that. Elephants in India are worth too much to shoot. They can be sold to circuses and park menageries.

But, better than this, the elephants in India do much work. They pull great wagons, that many horses could not move, and they work in lumber yards, piling up the big, heavy logs of teakwood, from which those queer, Chinese carved tables and chairs are made, and which wood is also used in ships. The Indians teach the elephants how to pile up big logs very carefully, and so straight that a big pile may be made without one falling off. Besides this the rich men of India, the Princes, own many elephants, which they ride on in little houses, called howdahs which are strapped to the backs of the big animals.

But before the wild elephants can be used thus they must go to school, to learn to be gentle, and to do as their drivers, or mahouts, tell them to do. And so Umboo went to school and I shall tell you about that.

Of course it was not such a school as you boys go to, and the big elephant boy did not have to learn to read and write. But he had to learn the meaning of Indian words, so that when he heard them he would know which meant go to the right or which to the left, and which meant to stand still, to kneel down or to go forward.

But I am getting a little ahead of my story. Umboo was still in the stockade trap with the other elephants. And there they were kept two or three days, without anything to eat or anything to drink. Fast they were kept in the stockade, where they could not get out, and as the days passed, and they felt very badly at not having anything to eat, or anything to drink, the elephants grew more quiet. No longer did they rush at the fence, and fall into the ditch. They huddled together in the middle part, and rubbed their trunks against one another, as men, in trouble, might shake hands.

"Oh, will we ever get out of this, and have sweet bark and palm nuts to eat again?" asked Umboo. "It was almost better to be lost in the jungle, as I was, than it is to be here, for then I had enough to eat. But of course I was lonesome without you," he said to his mother. "But I am hungry now."

"Perhaps they will let us out, or feed us soon," she said.

And, a little while after this, a noise was heard at the strong gate of the trap. It was slowly opened, but the elephants that were caught did not rush out. They feared more danger.

And then, to the surprise of Umboo and the others, in through the gate came great big elephants, and on the tops of their heads sat men, dressed in black clothing. And the men had strong ropes in their hands.

As soon as Tusker saw these men, and smelled them, he cried through his trunk:

"Ho, Brothers! Here is danger indeed! I smell the man-smell, even though it comes with other elephants like ourselves. We must get away from the danger!"

Tusker rushed at the gate, but before he could reach it two of the new elephants, who were tame, hurried toward him. The men on their heads threw the big ropes about Tusker, and he was pulled by the two elephants over toward a tree in the stockade, where he was made fast.

Tusker tried, with all his strength to break the ropes, but they only slipped easily around the tree, from which the bark had been taken to make it smooth and slippery for this very purpose.

"Be quiet, big, wild elephant," said one of the tame ones with a man on his head. "Be quiet and tell your friends to be quiet also. No one will hurt them. They will have food to eat, and sweet water to drink, if they are quiet."

Tusker heard this, and so did some of the other wild elephants. They were hungry and thirsty.

"Will you give us water to drink?" asked Tusker, for his trunk and mouth were very dry.

"You shall have water enough to swim in," answered one of the keonkies, or tame elephants.

"And may we eat?"

"You shall have all the palm nuts you want. That is if you are quiet."

"Then," said Tusker to Umboo, and the other wild elephants, "we may as well take it easy and be quiet. Raging about will do us no good, and we must eat and drink."

So most of the wild elephants became quiet. Some of them still tore around, trumpeting, but the big tame elephants pulled them with ropes to the trees where they were made fast. Mrs. Stumptail, and the other mother elephants, soon calmed down, and the boys and girls, like Umboo and Keedah, did as their mothers did.

In a short time the wild elephants were all either tied fast to trees, or were led away between two of the tame ones. Umboo was taken away from his mother.

"Oh, where am I going?" he cried to the tame elephants, one on either side of him. "I want to stay with you, Mother! Where are you taking me?"

"Do not make such a fuss, elephant boy," spoke one of the tame ones. "You will come to no harm, and you will see your mother again. You are going to go to school. You are young, and you will learn much more easily than some of the big elephants. Also you will have good things to eat and water to drink. Be nice now, and come with us."

Umboo had to go along whether he wanted to or not, for the big, tame elephants would pull him by the ropes. They led him to a sort of stable, and there he found some green fodder, some palm nuts and a tub of water. And Umboo drank the water first, for he was very thirsty. Then he ate and he felt better, though he wondered what had become of his mother.

But he did not wonder long, for elephants, and other animals, are not like boys and girls. They grow up more quickly, and get ready to go about for themselves, getting their own food, and living their own lives. And Umboo was big enough, now, to get along without his mother.

"Were you once living in the jungle, as I was?" asked Umboo of Chang, which was the name of one of the tame elephants.

"Surely," answered Chang, "I was as wild as Tusker, your big herd-leader. But when I was caught in the trap, as you were, and sent to school, I found the life here was much easier than in the jungle. It is true I have to do as the mahouts tell me, but they treat me kindly, they feed me and I never have to go thirsty, and when my toe nails get too long they smooth them down for me with a rough brick. Also they scrub my skin to keep away the biting bugs. You will like it here, Umboo, and soon you will go to school and learn how to pile the teakwood logs."

"And will I ride men on my head?" asked Umboo.

"Yes, you will learn to do that, and many things more," said Chang. But even he did not know all the wonderful things that were to happen to Umboo, nor how he was to go in the circus.

CHAPTER XII

UMBOO IS SOLD

Umboo, the big elephant boy, did not at once begin to learn the teakwood log-piling lesson. Just as in school you do not learn to read the first day, so it was with Umboo. He had to be trained by his keeper and the keonkies, or tame elephants.

And, after the first feeling of being sorry at having been taken away from his mother, Umboo grew to like the new life. His mother was sent to another big stable, farther away, though Umboo saw her once in a while. With him, however, were many of the wild elephants he had known when the herd was in the jungle. Keedah was one of these elephants.

"I don't like it here at all!" snarled Keedah, when he had been led up beside Umboo, a few days after they had all been caught in the trap. "I don't like it, and I'm not going to stay!"

"What are you going to do?" asked Umboo.

"I am going to run away," said the elephant boy, whom Umboo had once, in fun, knocked into the river. "I am going to run away, and go out in the jungle."

"Oh, no. I wouldn't do that if I were you," quietly said one of the tame elephants, coming up behind Keedah just then, and the half-wild elephant was so surprised that he nearly dropped a wisp of hay he was eating.

"If you ran away we should have to run into the jungle after you," went on the tame elephant. "And when we brought you back you would not have a nice time. It is better to do as you are told, and to learn to do what the black and white men tell you. For then you will be kindly treated, and have plenty to eat. And the work you will learn to do, after you go to school, as you and Umboo will go, will not be hard. Take my advice and stay where you are."

"Well, I guess I'll have to," said Keedah, with a funny look at Umboo. "I didn't know he heard me," he whispered, as if the tame elephant were a teacher in school, which, in a way, he was.

And then began long days and months of lessons for Umboo and the other wild elephants. They were not wild any longer, for the first thing they learned was that the tame elephants would help them, and next that the white and black men would be kind to them and feed them. So the jungle elephants, who used to roam about with Tusker for their leader, lost most of their wildness, quieted down, and were sent to different places in India to work in the lumber yards, or to carry Princes on their backs.

Umboo and his mother had to say good-bye, but they hoped to meet again, and though for a time Umboo felt sad, he soon forgot it as he had many things to learn.

One of the first was to let a man come near him to pat his trunk, and to feed him. In the beginning Umboo was very much afraid, because he smelled the man-smell, which Tusker had so often said meant danger. But Umboo grew to know that not all men were dangerous. For, though some might be hunters, with guns and sharp arrows, those who had caught the wild elephants were kind to the big animals.

"I wonder why I am afraid of the man?" thought Umboo. "He is much smaller than I am. His head hardly comes up to my tusks, and some of the tame elephants are even larger than I. Why are we so afraid of the men as to do just as they tell us?"

Of course Umboo did not know, but it is because man, who is also an animal, is put in charge of all the beasts of the jungle, the woods and fields. Animals are given to help man, and to feed him. And as a man has more brains—that is he is smarter than animals—he rules over them. Thus it is that even great elephants, and savage lions and tigers, as well as horses, know that man is their master, and must do as he wants them to.

So, though he could see that he was larger than a man, Umboo did not think much farther than this, and so he never made up his mind that, if he wanted to, he could run away, and that no one man could hold him. But perhaps it was just as well as it was, and that the elephant remained gentle and did as he was told, not trying to use his great strength against his friends.

One of the first things Umboo learned was to walk along, when he was told to do so in the Indian language.

At first Umboo did not know what this word meant. But his keeper gently pricked him with a sharp hook, called an "ankus," and to get away from the prick, which was like the bite of a big fly, Umboo stepped out and walked away.

"Ha! That is what I wanted you to do, little one," said the Indian, speaking to Umboo as he might to a child. And indeed the Indian mahouts consider their elephants almost like children.

When Umboo had learned that a certain word meant that he was to walk along, he was taught two others, one of which meant to go to the left, and the other to go to the right. Then, in a few weeks, he learned a fourth word, which meant to stand still, and then a fifth one, which meant to kneel down.

And though, at first, the elephant boy did not like doing the things he was told to do, as well as he had liked playing about in the jungle, he soon grew to see that his life was easier than it had been with Tusker and the others.

He never had to hunt for food, as it was brought to him by the keepers. Nor was he ever thirsty. And, best of all, he never had to drop what he was eating and run away, crashing through the jungle, because Tusker, or some other elephant had trumpeted the call of:

"Danger! I smell the man-smell!"

Umboo was used to the man-smell now, and knew that no harm would come to him. He knew the men were his friends.

And so he who had once been a wild baby elephant, grew to be a tame, big strong beast, who could carry heavy teakwood logs on his tusks, and pile them in great heaps near the river, where they were loaded upon great ships. Umboo did not know the boats were ships, but they were, and soon he was to have a ride in one. But I have not reached that part of his story yet.

Sometimes, instead of being made to pile the logs in the lumber yard, Umboo would be taken into the forest, where the Indians cut the trees down. The forest was something like the jungle where the boy elephant had once lived with Tusker and the others, and where he had played, and once been lost.

In the forest were great trees of teakwood and these the elephant workers had to drag out so they could be loaded upon carts, with great wooden wheels, and brought to the river. One day Umboo and Keedah were taken together to the teak forest.

"Now is our chance, Umboo," said the other elephant after a while as they went farther and farther into the woods. "Now is our chance!"

"Our chance for what?" asked Umboo, speaking in elephant talk, of course, and which the Indian keepers did not always understand.

"This is our chance to run away and go back to the jungle," went on Keedah. "When the men are not looking, after we have hauled out a few big logs, we will go away and hide. At night we can run off to the jungle."

"No," said Umboo, shaking his trunk, "I am not going to do it. If we run away they will find us and bring us back. Besides, I like it in the lumber yard. It is fun to pile up the big logs, and lay them straight."

"Pooh! I don't think so," said Keedah, who had not given up all his wild ways. "I am going to run!"

And so, watching his chance, when the Indian men were not looking, Keedah sneaked off into the dark part of the woods. In a little while he was missed, and the keepers, with shouts, started after him. They tied Umboo to a tree with chains, leaving him there while they went to hunt Keedah.

"They need not have chained me," thought Umboo. "I would not run away.

I like my men friends too much, for they are good to me."

The keepers got other elephants and hunted Keedah in the forest. For three days they searched for him, and at last they found him and brought him back. For Keedah had forgotten some of his wildness, and did not know so well how to keep away from the men who were after him, as he had known when he lived in the herd, with Tusker to lead the way.

So Keedah, tired and dirty, and hungry too, it must be said—for he had not found good things to eat in the woods—Keedah was brought back. And he was kept chained up for a week, and given only water and not much food. This was to tame him down, and make him learn that it did not pay to run off when he was taken to the teakwood forest.

"I wish I had done as you did, and stayed," said Keedah sorrowfully to

Umboo. "I am not going to run away any more."

So Umboo and the other wild elephants who were caught at the same time as he was, stayed around the lumber camp, and did work for their white and black masters. Sometimes a few of the elephants were sold, and taken away by Indian Princes, to live in stables near the palaces, to have gold and silver cloths fastened on their backs, and then the howdahs, in which rode the rich Indians, would be strapped on.

Sometimes other wild elephants were brought in, having been caught as Umboo had been. And once Umboo helped to tame one of these little wild ones, telling him to be nice, as he would be kindly treated and have food and water.

And one day new adventures came to Umboo.

By this time he was a big, strong elephant, nearly fully grown, for it was now many years since he had been a baby in the jungle. And one day, as he was standing near a pile of lumber, that he had helped to build, one of the white men, whom he knew, and who had been kind to Umboo, took a handkerchief from his white, linen coat pocket, and wiped his face, for the day was hot.

Then a little spirit of mischief seemed to enter Umboo. And this little spirit, or fairy, seemed to whisper:

"Take his handkerchief out of his pocket with your trunk, Umboo, and make believe wipe your own face with it. That will be a funny little trick, and will make the men laugh, and maybe they will give you some soft, brown sugar." This the elephants like very much.

Umboo saw the edge of the handkerchief sticking out of the man's pocket. Very softly the elephant reached put his trunk and took it. Then Umboo flourished the piece of white linen in the air, as the man had done, and pretended to use it, though Umboo's face was much larger than the man's, and really needed no handkerchief.

The man turned around, as he heard his friends laughing, and when he saw what Umboo had done the man smiled and said:

"Ha! That elephant is too smart to be piling lumber. I heard the other day where I could sell one to go in a circus. I'll sell Umboo! He will make a good circus elephant, to do tricks."

And so Umboo was sold, though at first he did not know what that was, nor where he was to be taken. He only thought of how the men laughed when he took out the handkerchief from the pocket.

CHAPTER XIII

UMBOO ON THE SHIP

The man who bought Umboo was one who owned part of a circus. He traveled about in India, and other far-off countries, looking for strange animals that he could send to America, across the ocean, where they would be put in cages and tents and shown to boys and girls, and also grown-up folk. You may think a circus is all fun and peanuts and pink lemonade, but it also teaches us something. Without a circus many boys and girls would never know what an elephant looks like; or a lion, or tiger or camel, except, perhaps, by pictures.

"And I'll send this trick elephant over to a circus," said the man who had bought Umboo from the lumber yard. "I think he will be a smart elephant, and make the boys and girls laugh." He knew Umboo liked boys and girls, for many of them had ridden on his back as he worked in the lumber yard.

"I thought Umboo was smart as soon as I saw him take the handkerchief from my pocket," said the lumber man to the circus man. "That is why I sent for you to let you buy him. For I knew you wanted a smart, young elephant for your circus."

"Yes, I am glad to get Umboo," spoke the circus man. "I wonder if he will do that handkerchief trick again? I'll try him."

So the circus man stood near our elephant friend, and let the end of his handkerchief stick a little way out of his pocket.

Umboo knew at once what was wanted of him.

"I'll just pull that white rag out and hear the men laugh," thought the elephant boy to himself. "I don't know why they think it is so funny, but I'll do it. I guess they would think it more funny if they could have seen me knock Keedah into the river."

Umboo reached out his trunk, when the man's back was turned toward him, and gently took out the handkerchief. Then the big elephant boy pretended to wipe his face with it.

"Ha! Ha!" laughed the circus man. "That is a good trick! I must give the elephant a big lump of sugar."

He did so, and Umboo liked it very much, letting the sweet juice trickle down his throat.

"I wish they would give me sugar every time I take out the white rag," thought Umboo. "It's fun!"

After this Umboo did not pile lumber any more. He was taken out of the yard, and kept by himself in a small stable, and given nice things to eat until one day the circus man opened the door and called:

"Well, Umboo, I guess we are ready to start now. You are going to say good-bye to India and to the jungle. You are going where Jumbo went — off to America to be in a circus show!"

Of course Umboo did not understand all that the circus man said to him, but the elephant boy thought to himself:

"Well, he is kind to me. He gives me sugar. I'll go with him, and pull that white rag out of his pocket as often as he lets me. I wonder what he was saying about Jumbo?"

For Umboo remembered hearing the other elephants talking about Jumbo, who, however, came from Africa and not from India.

"Come, Umboo!" called the circus man. "You are going on a big ship, and take a long ride. I hope you will not be seasick."

Umboo did not know exactly what a ship was. He had seen big boats come up the river, near where he worked, to get lumber, and some of the elephants, who had been down near the ocean shore, said those boats were ships. And of course Umboo did not know what it meant to be seasick.

However he liked the circus man, and when the elephant boy came out of the stable he felt around with his trunk in the man's pocket.

"For," thought Umboo, "if I pull that white rag out of his coat again, maybe he'll give me some more sweet sugar."

So, with the tip of his trunk, which could pick up little things, even as you can with your fingers, Umboo felt about for the handkerchief. He did not find it, however.

"Ha! Ha!" laughed the circus man, "You did not forget, did you? You are going to be a good trick elephant, I'm sure. Here is my handkerchief, in my other pocket. I put it there to fool you!" and he turned about so that the white cloth could be seen hanging down on the other side of his coat.

"Ha! That's funny!" thought Umboo. "I did not know the man had two pockets!"

Then the elephant pulled out the handkerchief again, and the man laughed and gave him a extra large lump of sugar.

"Now come with me, Umboo," said the man, and he led him away, out of the lumber yard.

"Where are you going?" called Keedah, and some of the other boys.

"I don't know," answered Umboo, in elephant talk, of course. "But I heard the man say something about making me do tricks in a circus."

"Oh, then you are going to have a fine, time," said one of the keonkies, or tame elephants, that help train the wild ones. "If you go to the circus you will have fun. A friend of mine was once in one, and then, in his old age, he came back to India to live. And he said he never enjoyed himself so much as in a circus. And how he did used to talk about the peanuts!"

"What are peanuts?" asked Umboo.

"I don't know," answered the keonkie, "but Zoop—that the was the name of my friend—said they were almost as good as the sweet sugar and palm nuts."

"Then they must be very good," said Umboo, "and I shall like them. Good-bye, friends!" he called. "Maybe some day I'll come back from the circus."

"But you never did; did you?" asked Snarlie the tiger, who, with the other animals in the tent, was listening to Umboo's story. "You never did go back, for you are here yet."

"No, I haven't gone back to India, and I don't believe I ever shall," spoke Umboo. "Sometimes I wish I could go back in the jungle for a little while, and get a few palm nuts, but the peanuts here are just as good, and there is never any danger."

"Please go on with your story," begged Horni, the rhinoceros. "I want to hear how you got over here, and joined the circus."

"I came on a ship, just as you did," answered Umboo, and then he went on to tell how he was led away from the lumber yard.

To get from the place where he had, for a year or more, been piling up teakwood logs, to the great, salt ocean which the ships crossed, Umboo had to take a ride on the railroad. He might have walked, but this would have taken too long.

Umboo had never before seen a railroad, a railroad car or a locomotive, and when he first noticed the big, black engine, puffing out smoke and steam, the elephant boy was as frightened as when he had seen the snake in the jungle. Umboo raised his trunk in the air, and made a loud trumpet sound of danger.

"Don't be afraid," said a tame elephant near by. "There is nothing to hurt you."

"Nothing to hurt me!" cried Umboo. "What do you call that big, black thing, whose breath steams out of the top of his head, as mine sometimes comes out of my trunk on a cold morning? Nothing to be afraid of? Why, that is worse than a big rhino! Much worse!"

"That is the engine, and it will give you a nice ride," said the tame elephant. "It will pull you along the shiny rails, and you will never have to lift your foot. Go close up to it, and see that it will not hurt you. Don't be afraid!"

Umboo trembled, but the circus man spoke kind words to him, and then the elephant walked slowly up to the engine, or locomotive. It snorted and puffed and tooted its whistle, and at each new sound Umboo started back, and would have run away. But the man spoke to him, and the tame elephant talked to him, and finally Umboo saw that the engine did not get off the shiny rails.

"Well, if it stays on them it can't chase after me," thought Umboo. "I can run to one side, but that big, black animal, that puffs steam out of the top of its head, can't. I guess I'll be all right."

Then Umboo was led past the engine, (which, of course, did him no harm) up a sort of little bridge of wood—a runway—that went from the ground into a big freight, or box car. At first Umboo feared this bridge might break with him, as he was so heavy, and an elephant doesn't like to step on anything that will give way and let him fall.

So Umboo first tried it with one foot, and then with another, and, finding it would not break, he stepped on it and walked into the car. There was plenty of straw in it, so Umboo would not be hurt if the car jolted as it rumbled along over the railroad tracks, and inside his new stable the elephant boy found some sweet roots and palm nuts.

He was so interested in eating these that, at first, he did not notice when the train started, and before he knew it Umboo found himself being pulled along without having to take a step.

"Ha!" thought the elephant. "It's just as the keonkie told me, I can move without lifting a foot! I am having a fine ride!"

Two days later Umboo reached the seashore and was led from the railroad car, and over to a big ship that was waiting in the harbor. To Umboo it looked more like a big house than a ship, and when they took him to the gang-plank, or another run-way, as they had taken him to the one that led into the freight car, he was again afraid something would break and let him fall. But when he tried it with his fore-feet, and found it firm, up it he walked and soon he was in a sort of stable, on board the big ship.

To his surprise, Umboo found other elephants there also, and from various parts of the ship came the smell of many different wild animals—camels, sacred cows from India, a rhinoceros, a buffalo and many strange beasts.

For this was a circus ship, and was bringing to America many strange birds and animals from the jungle.

"Now, Umboo, we are off!" said the circus man, as he came down to see the elephants and other creatures. "You are all going to start across the ocean in this big ship, and I hope none of you will be seasick."

Of course Umboo and the other elephants did not understand exactly what the man said, but they knew he was kind to them, for he gave them some food to eat and water to drink.

Pretty soon the ship began to pitch and toss and roll. It was out on the big ocean. The elephants did not so much mind the rolling motion, as they never stopped swaying themselves, and they were used to it, but some of the other animals had a bad time.

I wish I could tell you all that happened on board the ship, that was taking Umboo to the circus, but I have not room in this book. I'll tell you one thing that happened, though, and Umboo often used to laugh about it later.

One day, when the ship had been sailing about a week, a man came down in the hold, or stable where the elephants were. This man was a sort of joker. He liked to play tricks on animals and sometimes on his friends, and this time he thought he would play a trick on Umboo.

The man took a sour lemon, and plastered it all on the outside with some sticky brown sugar. This he held out to Umboo, saying:

"Here; have a nice, sweet lump!"

Of course Umboo thought it was all sugar, but when he chewed it, and found inside a sour lemon, it made tears come into his eyes, and he curled his trunk, and made such a funny, wrinkled face, that the man laughed and exclaimed:

"Oh, see how the elephant likes a lemon! Isn't that a funny trick!"

But I don't think it was a funny trick at all, and neither did Umboo. As soon as he could do so, he let the sour lemon drop out of his mouth into the straw on which he stood.

"Ha!" said the elephant next to Umboo. "If I could reach that man I'd tickle him with my trunk, and maybe pinch him, too."

"So would I," said Umboo. "But I can't reach him," and he could not, for the elephant was chained fast to the wall of the ship.

"But I'll know him when I see him again," exclaimed Umboo, "and the next time he comes near me maybe I can play a trick on him."

"I hope you can," said the other elephant.

And now you wait and see what happened.

The ship sailed on and on over the sea, each day coming nearer and nearer to America, which is the land of the circus. And Umboo and the other animals grew tired of being kept below decks, in the darkness. They wanted to get out into the sunshine.

Each day Umboo kept watch for the man who had given him the lemon in the lump of sugar, but the trick-player did not again come down where the elephants were.

And finally, one day, the circus man came down. He quietly rubbed the trunk of Umboo, patted him, and spoke kind words to him, feeding him good sugar.

"Now, my trick elephant," he said, "we will soon be going ashore, and we will see how you like a circus."

CHAPTER XIV

UMBOO IN THE CIRCUS

Many things happened to Umboo after he was taken out of the ship in which he had crossed the ocean. And there were so many of them that he could not remember all of them to tell his circus friends who were listening to his story.

"But did you get seasick?" asked Humpo, the camel. "That's what I want to know. Did you get seasick?"

"No, I did not," answered Umboo. "But I was tired of staying in the dark part of the ship so long. I wanted to get out in the sun. And I wanted to see if I could do that trick again, of taking the white rag from the man's pocket."

"And did you?" asked Snarlie, the tiger.

"I did, the first chance I had," answered Umboo. "But that was not until I had been off the ship for a day or so."

Umboo and the other animals were taken from the ship, and again put in railroad cars to be taken to a sort of training place. Wild animals, fresh from the jungle, are not taken at once to the circus. If they were the lions would roar, the tigers would snarl and the elephants would try to break loose and run away, and this would so scare the boys and girls who went to the circus that they would never come again.

So circus men first send the animals to a sort of training camp. There is one in Bridgeport, Conn., and another in New Jersey, on the Hackensack meadows. There the wild beasts are taken in charge, by men who know how to train them.

And it was to a place like this that Umboo was taken. It was not at all like a circus, except for the number of wild animals about. There was no big white tent; nothing but a sort of large barn, and there were no gay flags fluttering, and no bands playing music. All that would come later.

Umboo was chained in the middle of the barn, with the other elephants, and some hay was given him to eat. At first the elephant, who, not long before, had been wild in the jungle, and later piling teakwood logs, was uneasy and a bit frightened. So were his companions.

"But don't be afraid, Umboo," said the kind man who had come all the way from India with the elephant. "You will soon like it here, though you may not like being taught tricks. But you will like it when you can do funny things, and make the boys and girls laugh. Also, when you do your tricks well, you shall have lumps of sugar."

"Well, I hope there will be no lemons inside the lumps," said Umboo to

Char, another big beast next to him.

"What is that about lemons in sugar?" asked Char.

"Oh, a man on the ship played a trick on me," answered Umboo. "I haven't seen him since, but I am on the lookout for him, and when I do see him, if I get near enough—well, I'll make him wish he hadn't fooled me."

"It was a mean trick," said Char. "I hope you find that man."

For a few days the elephants, and other wild jungle animals, who were to be tamed and taught to do things in the circus, were left to themselves. This was to get them quiet after their long trip, and to make them feel at home.

Umboo did not have to be tamed, for he was already kind and gentle. But some of the lions and tigers were fierce and wild, and they had to get to know that the circus men would not harm them. Most of the elephants, like Umboo, were no longer wild, but they knew nothing about being trained to do tricks. None of them could even so much as take a handkerchief out of a man's pocket, so really Umboo was one class ahead of them. But that did not make him proud.

One day, about a week after he had come to the circus-barn, Umboo saw some men coming toward him with ropes and other things. Among the men was the one from India, and this man Umboo liked.

"Now, Umboo" said this man, "you are going to learn a harder trick than that of taking a handkerchief from my pocket. You are going to learn to stand on your hind legs. It may seem hard to you at first, but it is easy when you know how, and you will like it. The boys and girls who come to the circus to see you, will like it, too, and you will get sugar if you do the trick well."

Of course Umboo did not know all that the man said to him, but he understood that something new was going on, and he reached out his trunk to touch his friend.

"I haven't any sugar for you now," said the man with a laugh, "but I may have some later. Let me see how you behave."

The men began putting ropes around Umboo's big neck. He did not mind this, for it had been done before, in India, when he was to pull a heavy wagon of teakwood logs. But this time it was different.

All of a sudden Umboo felt his front legs being lifted from the ground. His head and trunk went up in the air, and all his weight came on his hind legs. They were strong enough to bear it, but the elephant did not know what was going on.

"It's all right, my elephant friend!" said the man from India. "Up!

Up! Stand up! Stand on your hind legs, Umboo!"

And Umboo had to do this whether he wanted to or not. The rope, on which the men were pulling, and which was fast to a hook in the ceiling of the barn over head, was lifting Umboo's front feet from the ground. This left him only his hind legs, and he had to stand on them whether he wanted to or not.

If you have ever tried to teach your dog to stand on his hind legs, you will know what was being done to Umboo. When you try to teach your dog this trick, you generally take him where he can stand up in a corner, so he can lean against the wall and will not fall over backwards or sideways; for that is what he feels like doing when you lift up his front legs.

But an elephant is so big, you see, that it would take a very large corner for him to back into. And he is so big and heavy that not even ten men could lift up his front legs. So they just hitch a rope around his head, and then men, hauling on the rope and pulleys, lift the front of the elephant, as men hoist up a piano.

"Ugh!" grunted Umboo through his trunk, as he felt his head and front legs going up. "What in the world is this?"

"Don't be afraid, my jungle friend," said an old big, tame elephant, who was kept in the circus barn just to make the others feel more at home. "Don't be afraid. You are only being taught the first of your tricks. I was taught the same way. It won't hurt you. Here, throw your weight on your back legs, and stand on them—this way."

And, to the surprise of Umboo, the other elephant, without the help of any ropes, reared himself up in the air and stood on his hind legs just as your dog can do.

"That's the way to do it!" said the trick elephant.

"I wonder if I can?" said Umboo.

"Try it," urged his new friend.

And when the man loosed the ropes, and let Umboo's front legs down, after they had hoisted them up once, he suddenly gave a little spring, and up he went, standing on his hind legs all by himself, and almost as good as the trick beast could do it.

"Well, I declare!" cried one of the men. "That elephant is the smartest one we ever trained. He does the trick after being shown just once!"

"Oh, yes, I knew he was smart when he did that handkerchief trick," said the man from India. "Umboo will be ready to join the circus before any of the others."

Once more Umboo was hoisted up by the ropes, but there was really no need for it. He knew what was wanted of him, and he did it.

"That's fine!" said the big elephant. "If you learn the other things as easily as you learned this trick, you will have no trouble."

"Are there other tricks to learn." asked Umboo.

"Oh, many of them," answered Wang, the best trick elephant in the circus. "You have only just begun."

And Umboo found that this was so. In the ten days that followed he was taught many more tricks. Some of them he did not learn so easily as he had the one of standing on his hind legs, and the ropes had to be used many times. But the other trick elephants, of whom there was more than one, showed the untrained ones what to do, and, in time, Umboo and his friends could go through many "stunts," as the circus men called them.

Umboo learned to lie down and "play dead," he learned to stand on a little stool, like an over-turned washtub, he learned to kneel down over a man stretched on the ground, and not crush him with the great body, weighing more than two tons of coal.

Other tricks, which Umboo learned, were to take pennies in his trunk, lift up a lid of a "bank," which was a big box, drop the pennies in and ring a bell, as if he had put money in a cash drawer. He also learned to turn the handle of a hand organ with his trunk, to ring a dinner bell, and do many other tricks, such as you have seen elephants do in a circus.

Then, one day, the man from India came where Umboo was, and giving him some peanuts, which our friend had learned to like very much, said:

"Well, now it is time you joined the circus. You know enough tricks to make a start, and your circus-trainer will teach you more. So off to the circus you go, Umboo! Off to the circus!"

And the next day Umboo went.

CHAPTER XV

UMBOO REMEMBERS

Brightly in the sun gleamed the white tents. In the wind the gay flags fluttered. Here and there were men selling pink lemonade and peanuts. Around the green grass were the big wagons—wagons that needed eight or ten horses to pull, wagons shining with gold and silver mirrors—heavy, rumbling wagons, which Umboo and the other elephants had to push out of the mud when the horses could not pull them.

"And so this is the circus, is it?" asked Umboo, as his friend, Wang, and he were led up to the tents.

"This is the circus," spoke Wang. "But I forgot. This is your first one; isn't it?"

"The very first," answered Umboo. "My! It's lots different from the barn where I learned my tricks, isn't it?"

"Oh, yes, heaps different. It's more jolly," said Wang.

"And it's different from the jungle," went on Umboo.

"Oh, yes indeed! It isn't at all like the jungle," said Wang. "I remember the jungle very well. I always had to be sniffing here and there for danger, and often I had to drink muddy water, or else I went hungry. Here that never happens. All we have to do here is to perform our tricks, push a wagon out of the mud now and then, and eat and sleep. You'll like it here, Umboo."

"I'm sure I shall," he answered. "But what is that funny noise?"

"That is the music playing," answered Wang. "In the circus we do our tricks to band music. It's more fun that way."

Umboo liked the music, and there was one man who played a big horn—larger than himself, and the horn went: "Umph-umph!" just as Tusker used to trumpet through his trunk.

Umboo and the other elephants were taken into the animal tent, and placed around the outer ring, their legs chained to stakes driven in the ground. In cages were monkeys, lions, tigers and other beasts of the wood or jungle.

"Was it this circus of ours which you were first taken to, Umboo?" asked Humpo. "I came here about a year ago."

"No, it was not this one, but it was one like it," said the elephant.

"I came here about a year ago."

"I remember that time," said Snarlie. "I liked you as soon as I saw you, Umboo."

"So did I," spoke Woo-Uff, the lion, stretching out his big paws.

"Let us hear the rest of Umboo's story," suggested Chako, the monkey.

"Did you like the circus?"

"Indeed I did, very much," Umboo answered.

Then he told how he stood in the ring, and watched the boys and girls, and the men and women, come in to look at the animals before they went in the main tent, to sit down and watch the performers and animals do their tricks and "stunts."

Boys and girls, and some grown-folk, too, gave the elephants peanuts and bits of popcorn balls which the big fellows liked very much, indeed.

While Umboo was standing in line, with the other elephants, waiting until it was time for them to go in the big tent, and perform their tricks, such as standing on their hind legs and getting up on small barrels, our jungle friend saw a man coming toward him with a bag in his hand.

And, all at once Umboo remembered something. He looked sharply at the man and thought:

"Ha! There is the fellow who gave me the sour lemon inside the lump of sugar. Now is my chance to play a trick on him."

The man, with the bag in his hand, walked toward Umboo. To that man all elephants looked alike. He did not know he had ever seen this one before, and had played a mean trick on him. And the man said to another man who was with him:

"Watch me fool this elephant. I have an empty bag. I have blown it up full of wind, so that it looks like a bag of peanuts. I'll give it to this elephant and fool him."

"Maybe he'll bite you," said the other man, and the first one answered:

"Pooh! I'm not afraid. Watch me! I fooled an elephant once before. I gave him a lemon in some candy, and you should see the funny face he made. Ha! ha!"

"Ah, ha!" thought Umboo to himself. "He laughs, does he? Wait until I see what a funny face he is going to make."

The man held out the bag of wind to Umboo. But, instead of taking it, and getting fooled, the wise elephant suddenly dipped his trunk into a tub of water that stood near. Umboo sucked his trunk full of water and then, all at once, before the man knew what was going to happen, Umboo blew the water all over him.

"Whewiff!" went the water in the man's face, and all over his new suit, that he had put on to wear to the circus.

"Oh, my!" cried the man. "What happened?" and he spluttered and stuttered and gurgled. "What happened?" he asked, as he backed away and wiped the water from his face.

"I guess what happened," said the man who was with him, but who did not get wet, "was that the elephant played a trick on you, instead of you playing one on him. That's what happened!"

"I guess it did," said the man, whose windblown bag was all wet and flabby now. "But I don't see why he did it. I never fooled him before!"

"Maybe this is the same elephant you fooled with the lemon," said the second man.

"It couldn't be," spoke the wet one. "That was a long while ago, on a ship, and an elephant can't remember."

"But I did remember," said Umboo, as he told his story to his circus friends. "I could remember that man even now, if I saw him. And so I got even with him for giving me a lemon," and the big elephant laughed, until he shook all over like a bath-tub full of jelly.

"What happened after that?" asked Umboo.

"Oh, after that the man went out of the circus tent," said the elephant. "Everybody was laughing at him and the funny faces he made. But the water didn't hurt him much, and he soon dried for it was a hot day."

"And did you do your tricks in the circus?" asked Chako.

"Oh, yes, I went in the ring, and heard the music play. Then all us elephants stood on our hind legs, and I played the hand organ, rang a bell, put pennies in my bank and did many tricks. And one I did I liked best of all."

"What was that?" asked Horni, the rhinoceros.

"It was firing a little brass cannon," answered Umboo. "Some other elephants and myself played soldiers at war, and toward the end I had to pull a string with my trunk. In some way, I don't just know how, the string fired the cannon. None of the other elephants would do it. They were afraid, but I wasn't. I saw that the cannon wouldn't hurt me if I didn't get in front where its black mouth was, so I pulled the string. And when I did the cannon went 'Bang!' And the band played, and the big drum went 'Boom!' and the big horn went 'Umph-umph!' and the boys and girls yelled like anything. It was lots of fun!

"I liked that circus very much. I hope, someday, they'll let me shoot a cannon here."

"Maybe they will," said Woo-Uff, the lion. "I should like to hear it.

But is that all your story, Umboo?"

"That is all, yes. I stayed with that circus for some time, and then was sold again, and as you all know, brought here. And I like it here very much, because you are all so kind to me. And I enjoyed listening to the story you told, Woo-Uff, and to Snarlie's story also."

"Well, we liked yours," said Chako, the monkey, as he hung by his tail and ate a peanut.

"Is there any one else who can tell a story?" asked Snarlie. "We will soon be traveling on again, but after that, when we settle down to rest, I should like to hear another tale."

"I can tell about my jungle," said Chako.

"We have had enough of jungles," said Woo-Uff. "Does any circus animal know any other kind of stories?"

"How would you like to hear one about the hot, sandy desert?" asked Humpo, the camel.

"That would be fine!" cried Umboo. "Tell us your story, Humpo!"

"I will," promised the camel. And, if all goes well, that story will be in the next Circus Animal Book; if you think you would like to read it. It will be called "Humpo, the Camel."

The elephants swayed to and fro, their leg-chains clanking in the tent. The monkeys chattered among themselves. Snarlie, the big, striped tiger yawned and stretched. Woo-Uff, the lion, laughed.

"Ha! I wonder what makes that lion so jolly?" said one of the circus keepers.

"Perhaps the elephant tickled him," suggested a second man.

"Maybe he had a funny dream," spoke another.

"Both wrong!" said Woo-Uff, in animal language that the other circus beasts could understand. "I was laughing at the way Umboo squirted water on the lemon-man."

"Yes, that was funny," said Umboo. "Very funny!" And he, too, laughed as he chewed his hay.

And, now that his story is finished, we will say good-bye to him and his friends for a while.

THE END